The Farm

Vivian Bickell

Contents

One

P orter

The wind blew my shaggy brown hair around my eyes as I squinted into the field. I needed to get this cow back before this storm ruined all the chances I had left. If only the rest of those damn cows hadn't busted through my new fence, the one that cost basically my life savings. But I'd be damned if one cow was going to ruin my night. Especially when I know there's a cold beer waiting for me.

"Down on the right!" I yelled before nudging my horse Ace in the side. He instantly took off and I couldn't help but smile while feeling his sheer power beneath me. He sped off so fast he almost knocked the cowboy hat off my head, luckily it stayed on. The last thing I wanted to do was have to go shopping for a new one. One of the worst things in the world was shopping.

"Got eyes on the little shit," Jeremy's voice said behind me.

I didn't have to turn around to know where he was, I knew he was on my left. Nudging Ace in the side again, I raised the lasso above my head and just made it onto the cow before it could run away. Jeremy let out an excited whoop as the cow simply glared at me. Smug little bastard.

By the time we rode back to the farm the skies opened and heavy rain fell onto my body, completely soaking my thighs. These jeans will be fun to take off. With a sigh I hoisted myself out of the saddle and landed onto my feet, taking the cow into the barn with me. The rest of the cows simply looked up but didn't seem to care too much that their buddy had returned.

"How much do you think that fence will take to fix?" Jeremy asked as he started untacking our horses.

"Too damn much," I said while taking my wet cowboy off and brushing the hair out of my eyes.

He grumbled as well before his eyes looked over at me. It was very obvious that Jeremy and I were twins, we were pretty identical. We both had shaggy brown hair and a pair of green eyes we inherited from our father. If only he was still here today. Our mother was still around but she was a whole different mess. I'd always be grateful to have someone to connect to like Jeremy.

"What if we ask Kurt?"

"Dude," I said while sitting down onto a bale of hay. "We can't do that."

He gave me a look, the one Kurt used a lot, while his horse shook next to him. "Why not? This is still his ranch Port. And he still gets updated about everything and makes decisions." With a frown he glanced down at his hands before shoving them into his pockets. "He even said just because he's in the hospital nothing has changed."

The silence that followed made me frown as my eyes fell to the floor. Kurt was like a second father to us and having him be in the hospital made us both think about our father. I don't want to lose another parent. But I also didn't want Jeremy to be upset. While we may be twins, I was still older by ten minutes and had always been protective of him. Which was why I sighed and looked up at him while saying, "Fine. Let's go talk to him."

Jeremy finally smiled as I stood up and cracked my back. After the horses were put away and everything was taken care of we made our way inside the farmhouse. I instantly made a beeline over to the fridge and got one beer and a Coke out as our two dogs ran into the room.

"Heads up," I said before chucking the Coke over to Jeremy who instantly grabbed it. "Alright I'm done for the night. If another cow escapes don't wake me."

I heard a chuckle while leaving the kitchen and making my way upstairs, continuing to drink as I walked. Once in my bathroom I stripped down and turned the shower on, waiting until it heated up. My eyes wandered towards the mirror where I frowned. Damn, I need to shave. My hand ran over my scruffy face as the ink on my bicep made me look down. The two dates calmed me down before sliding into the shower and groaning from the heat.

The water slid down my back as my hands landed onto the tile, my aching muscles screaming for me to lay down. Usually my body reacted better but today I was really feeling my age. Not that twenty eight was old but days like these really made it feel ancient. As long as I had access to a hot shower at the end of the day, all the shit I put my body through will be worth it. When the water turned cold I turned the water off before running a towel over my body, chugging the rest of my beer.

Lightning lit up my room as I walked in which only made me sigh more. The pastures are going to be a fucking disaster tomorrow. But I knew Jeremy would push for us to go visit Kurt tomorrow. I wasn't sure which was worse- walking through the mud or asking the man I admire for money. Both sounded pretty awful. With that thought in mind I fell down onto the bed as my dog Sadie jumped up with me. Her body snuggled into mine as more lightning filled the room before my eyes finally shut.

*

"I don't know why you like that crap," I said while shoving the iced frape latte thing into Jeremy's waiting hands.

He laughed while practically cradling the cup in his hands before taking a sip. When the woman handed me my own black coffee I pulled away from the window, continuing the journey to the hospital. "It's so good though," he said in between more sips.

"You're literally drinking sugar."

"And you're literally drinking dirt."

I smirked while rolling my eyes as Jeremy turned some pop crap on the radio, singing along as he drank more of his sugar water. We might have the same face but that's pretty much where our similarities stopped. Besides being on the farm we didn't share same interests. Where I liked country music and whiskey, Jeremy liked thumpy pop music and fruity sugary drinks. I think it's pretty funny how different we are, being twins. I'm glad we aren't the same though, makes things more fun.

"God, this parking lot is like a lake," he said as I drove the truck through a large puddle before parking.

"I know, we got so much rain."

After drinking the rest of my coffee we walked inside the large building before getting into the elevator. The trip to Kurt's room was very familiar by now, since we came here every week. "Knock, knock," I said after ducking my head into the room.

Kurt instantly turned towards us and smiled as we walked over to his bed. "There's my boys," he said as his arms opened to give us hugs. Something I had always loved about him was how he had accepted us so easily into his life. He treated us like his actual sons since we were little. When our father died he was there to help us, and I was so glad he was.

"You look good," I said while pulling back so Jeremy could hug him.

"You really do," Jeremy said while sinking down onto the bed.

Kurt simply gave us a small smile while leaning back onto the pillows behind him. "You boys are just being nice." With a slight cough he slunk back into his pillow, his face looking a little pale. I hated seeing him in here all because of stupid cancer. Colon cancer can go fuck itself. Luckily it was caught in the early stage and he had been responding well to treatment. I needed him to get better though. There's no way I can lose another father.

"Porter doesn't know how to be nice." My eyes rolled as I slapped Jeremy upside the head, his gasp filling the room. He then laughed while shoving me back, Kurt smiling as he watched us.

"You know Jer's lying, I'm the nicest. Anyway," I said while sinking down on the opposite side of the bed. "How have you been? Any changes?"

He slowly shook his head before saying, "You mean since the last time you guys were here... two days ago? The only change is they swapped out my pudding for jello."

"Those monsters." Jeremy laughed when Kurt gave him a lazy smile.

"Now tell me, what's new at the farm?" When neither of us didn't say anything his smile fell as he looked between us. "Okay, what happened?"

When Jeremy looked over at me I sighed and ran a hand over my face. "There was a slight mishap with the new fence I had put in." When he simply gave me that 'dad' look I continued. "One of the cows busted through it and we're going to have to get it replaced."

"Porter."

"Not the whole fence, but a section."

"Porter."

"I didn't want to ask you because I know you put us in charge of the farm, and you're in the hospital. I really don't want to keep forcing you to spend money when you need it more and-"

When his hands grabbed mine, I finally stopped talking and looked into his gentle eyes. "Did you two think I was going to be mad about this? Boys, it's a farm. I know things break and I know animals can be little shits about things. You know that you two can always come to me with anything and I don't want you to think that just because I'm in here, anything is different. Money is fine; just tell me if you're spending ten thousand or more at a time. My bank just needs a heads up for large purchases. Okay?"

Jeremy looked over at me with a smile before he said, "Thanks Kurt."

"Seriously Kurt, thank you."

He gave both of our hands a squeeze before saying, "While I have you guys here, I just got word that my nephew will be coming from New York."

"New York?" Jeremy asked while raising his eyebrows. "I didn't know you had family outside of Iowa."

"My sister moved out there with her second husband. I think she's on number four now, but Levi is a good kid. I guess he's been in a rebellious state recently and my sister is shipping him out here. Honestly she should just talk to him but she doesn't listen to me."

Great, the last thing I need is to have to watch a rebellious kid. "How old is he exactly?"

"He's twenty four now. But I need you two to watch after him while he's here. I was informed that he's coming on Monday and he's staying at the farmhouse. So be good, but I know you two will be nice to him. He's a city boy and he hasn't been out to the farm since he was two."

Fuck, I thought with a sigh. City boys are always the worst. They never want to get their hands dirty. "Sounds fun," Jeremy said as he gave me a pointed look.

"Yeah, fun." About as fun as drilling screws into my eyes.

**

"Come on Port! They're going to be here any minute." My eyes lazily looked over at Jeremy, who was practically beaming by the door. He'd been weirdly excited ever since Kurt told us his nephew was coming.

"I'll pass." I grunted when he came over and pulled me off the couch.

He pulled me towards the door as I groaned, "Why are you so fucking happy about this?"

Once we were outside he leaned against the front porch, the porch light bouncing off his shaggy hair. His smile faded though as he looked out towards the driveway. "I just thought it might be fun to have someone new around." When he crossed his arms over his chest and looked down I frowned. "I'm not like you Porter, I'm not everyone's favorite person and I'm not the life of the party. I just thought I could maybe make this guy my friend, I don't really have a lot."

My frown deepened as I wrapped my arms around him and pulled him closer. "I'm your friend Jer."

"Doesn't count," he mumbled against my shirt. "You're my brother."

"Am I chopped liver to you?" He laughed against my body as his fingers tightened onto my back. "And just because we're twins, doesn't mean anything. Even if we weren't related you'd still be my best friend." He finally pulled back with an actual smile.

"Really?"

He laughed again from the look I gave him. "Yes really. You're a kickass person Jeremy and everyone loves you, give yourself more credit."

"So you'll be nice to this guy?"

"Only for you."

When he smiled again he hugged me before we both looked up at a cab driving our way. "Come on!" He happily said while grabbing my arm and pulling me down the stairs.

I leaned against the railing behind my body, Jeremy doing a little happy dance next to me. When the cab stopped I watched as the door opened and a blonde head appeared. The guy who stepped out looked like a city boy that's for sure. He had very tight jeans on, some fancy looking shoes and a shirt that probably cost more than my entire wardrobe. His big green eyes looked at the farmhouse with disgust before he finally looked at me. He might be hot which damn, he was, but city boys weren't my type.

When I looked over to Jeremy I was surprised to see his mouth slightly open, his cheeks pink. My eyes followed his to realize another guy got out of the cab. This guy was huge, and Jeremy and I were 6'1. He had to be 6'6, and had huge shoulders and biceps. His curly black hair was falling into his brown eyes, which were currently looking at my brother. Oh geez. I felt Jeremy slink behind me as the cab driver waved and drove off, leaving us with two strangers.

"Uh hey," I said while looking in between them. The small blonde was so short next to curly hair it was actually comical. "Kurt said only one person was coming?"

"I brought a friend," the blonde said as he looked around with disgust again.

"So you must be Levi."

Those green eyes looked up at me with a strange look before that bored look came back. "Yup."

The guy with black hair walked up and looked down at Jeremy, who was still hiding behind me. "Hi," his deep voice said as he held a hand out. "I'm Wyatt."

My eyebrows rose as I looked at Jeremy behind me to see his cheeks turning a darker shade of pink. His hand gripped Wyatt's larger one before whispering, "Jeremy." Wyatt smiled at him which only made Jeremy blush harder. Ugh god.

Wyatt glanced over at me before giving me a firm handshake. "Porter," I said while giving him a nod. "Well, this is the farm." They both looked around, Levi frowning more. "Do you know how long you guys are staying?"

"Until my mom wants me back," Levi said before grabbing some bags with fancy logos on them. When he walked closer I simply stared at him until he said, "Can you show me inside? I'm not staying outside the entire time."

Wyatt rolled his eyes before grabbing his own bags. "Oh uh, sure. Follow me."

When we walked in our dogs ran towards them, Wyatt loving on them but Levi quickly getting out of the way. Alright, strike two. City boys who don't like dogs? This just keeps getting worse and worse. The dogs followed me upstairs before I pointed towards two rooms. "Those two rooms are free; Jeremy and I have the other ones down the hallway."

"Great," Levi said before opening one of the doors before slamming it behind him.

Wyatt sighed as he looked at the closed door. "Levi has a lot of stress in his life right now; he's normally not this bitchy. Well, his level of bitchiness isn't usually so high."

"Have you guys been friends long?" Jeremy whispered, instantly blushing when Wyatt looked down at him.

"We're cousins, but he's been my best friend since we were little. We're six years apart but he's the brother I never had." His brown eyes then looked between us before a smile spread across his face. "It's crazy how much you two look alike."

I couldn't help but roll my eyes. "Yeah, being identical twins does that. Well, I guess that's everything. If you need anything just let me or Jer know. But just make yourself at home."

"Thanks."

He gave us another smile before going into the same room Levi wandered into, but luckily not slamming the door. When Jeremy floated down the stairs I followed him, watching him grab a Coke from the fridge. I simply leaned against the counter and waited for him to look over. When he finally did he jumped before squeaking, "What?"

"Oh don't play dumb. You have the hots for Wyatt."

His cheeks lit up again as he started digging through the pantry before coming back with chips. He always ate when he was nervous. "Shh! I do not have the hots for him Porter, I don't even know him. I know nothing about him okay? I'm sure he has a super hot girlfriend or boyfriend."

"Yeah, no. Did you see the way he was looking at you? He was practically undressing you with his eyes."

"Was not!" I laughed as he shoveled more chips into his mouth. "Anyway, they'll probably only be here for a little bit. So I'm just going to be nice to them and not ..."

"Think about his dashing brown eyes?"

"Yeah," he sighed before looking up at me. "Hey!"

I laughed when he ran after me, before shoving me onto the couch. Since he was still holding the chip bag, I easily took them and started up Netflix. We were currently watching some creepy show that he wanted to watch, but now I was weirdly into it. And even though there were two complete strangers upstairs, I didn't feel weird because Jeremy was next to me. We passed the chips back and forth as I tried to get those green eyes out of my mind.

Two

L^{evi}

"Please just take that pillow and hold it over my face." When I was met with silence I looked up to see Wyatt typing something on his phone, completely ignoring me. "Wyatt!"

Those brown eyes lazily looked over at me as he raised a black eyebrow. "Whining really isn't a good trait on you Lev. Seriously, just be happy that we're somewhere away from your awful mother and William."

I frowned while looking up at the ceiling as my hands landed onto my stomach. William and my mom had only been dating two months, but he was already trying to act like a father. A shitty one, but it was still annoying. I guess he was right but I still hated being shipped across the country. Since I was little I never felt like I belonged and people like my mother never understood what I was going through. She just likes to constantly tell me I'm stupid and don't know what I'm talking about.

"Thank you for coming with me."

Honestly I don't know what I'd do without Wyatt. He's been with me through literally everything and never judged me. That's what a true friend does but he's so much more than a friend. He's family and my favorite person in the world. Plus, he's the only one who can put up with me.

"You really think I'd let you come all the way here by yourself?"

When I went to say something snarky I saw he was still looking at his phone. With a sigh I got up and looked over his shoulder to see a picture of... what was his name? One of the twins.

"What are you doing?"

"I found Jeremy's Instagram, damn. Just look at his body."

I rolled my eyes while leaning my arms onto his ridiculous large shoulders and watched him scroll through pictures. "This is what you're doing? Stalking someone you just met literally two seconds ago?"

"Damn straight," he said while continuing to scroll.

I watched him click on a picture, the twins faces smiling back at us. They might be twins but I could tell a difference between them. Jeremy seemed like a sweet guy, a little shy. Porter seemed like the kind of guy to sing karaoke in a bar he just walked into. Ugh, whatever. I'm not going to get sucked into a rabbit hole of two attractive twins. I'd never be able to land someone like that anyway, not when he learns what I've always hid.

"You're ridiculous," I said while rolling my eyes and walking back over to the bed.

Once I fell onto the comfortable bed he looked up at me before holding his phone up. The photo showed Jeremy and Porter shirtless in a lake, holding up fishing poles with two pretty big fish. "Look at this picture and tell me they aren't gorgeous. Jeremy in particular."

"They have the same face Wyatt, and seems like the same bodies."

He was then turning his phone back around so he could stare at the picture again. "There's something about country boys that just make my mouth water. Fuck look at this," the next photo he was showing me was Jeremy in a cowboy hat sitting on top of a horse. "It could be in a magazine."

"My god, go take a cold shower or something. You just met him! He could have a girlfriend for all you know."

"Oh I plan on finding that out." When he saw me rolling my eyes he said, "I came across the country for you, let me have some fun."

Before I could respond he was back to Insta-stalking which only made me sigh. After staring up at the ceiling for god knows how long, I finally rolled off the bed and started unpacking my clothes. When I pulled out a yellow sweater I watched the bottle that was wrapped up inside fall to the floor. I shakily picked the bottle up and held it close to my chest. These pills were the only thing keeping me going.

"Hey," Wyatt's quiet voice said as he grabbed one of my hands. When I looked up at him he squeezed my hand before saying, "It's going to be okay. I promise."

With a nod I put the pills back into my bag before sitting back down onto the bed. I couldn't wait until I didn't need those anymore. But for now I was stuck inside a farmhouse in the middle of nowhere Iowa. I hated this.

*

The rest of the day I hung out in my room until Wyatt literally pulled me out and said I needed to eat. As we were walking down the stairs I could hear the sound of some kind of sports game playing. Once we were waltzing into the living room I saw Porter sitting on the couch drinking a beer. "Come on!" He yelled towards the TV. "Get a pair of fucking eyes ref." When he looked up and saw us he said, "Oh hey."

"Mind if we raid your kitchen?" Wyatt asked.

"Go for it. I actually ordered some pizzas a little while ago if you guys want some."

"Thanks man, what game you watching?"

I frowned when I watched Wyatt sit next to Porter, both talking about the sports game. When Wyatt gave me a look I frowned again before walking over and sitting down into a huge recliner. Since they were talking about the game I looked around the room and realized how homey it felt. My home had never felt like this before but it had never been a home. That was why my mother had such an easy time shipping me here.

After hearing a doorbell I heard someone run to the front door and all but body slam the door. A few moments later I watched a smiling Jeremy walking into the room. "Pizza is here! I-" He instantly stopped walking when he looked at Wyatt, who was also looking at him with interest.

"Let me help you," Wyatt said while standing up and taking the boxes out of Jeremy's hands.

"Oh uh, thank you." Jeremy was then nervously scratching his arm before he looked around the room. "I was just going to put them on the coffee table though."

Wyatt smiled while walking over to the coffee table before placing the boxes down. When he looked over at me he smiled when I rolled my eyes. Once the boxes were placed on the table Porter instantly opened one up and grabbed a piece of pepperoni pizza.

"Little shit," he suddenly growled at the TV. When I looked to see what he was upset about I saw a basketball game playing. Such a typical guy thing.

"Would anyone like anything to drink?" Jeremy asked as he smiled politely between us. "We have beer, water, Coke and maybe some tea."

Porter took a huge bite out of his pizza while saying, "Sugar water."

"Shut up." He was then looking at me with a soft smile. "Thirsty?"

Since Wyatt was standing behind him, he missed the way my friend completely stared at his ass when he asked that. Ugh. "Do you have sparkling water?"

His smile fell as he shook his head. "Sorry, just normal water."

"Fine."

"Wyatt?" He quietly asked while turning around. "Are you thirsty?"

"Parched," he said which only made me roll my eyes harder. "I'll have whatever you're having."

They stared at each other for a few more moments before Jeremy all but ran from the room, Wyatt still looking at him. When he came back he handed Wyatt a Coke and handed me a glass of water before sitting next to his brother. Wyatt was then handing me a piece of pizza before sitting next to Porter.

"So Levi," Jeremy said as I turned towards his smiling face. He was being really nice to a complete stranger. But maybe that was because I wasn't openly checking him out like Wyatt. "How's New York? Port and I have never been there."

I simply shrugged before saying, "Insanely busy, usually smells and people aren't the nicest. It's pretty weird to be out here, there's hardly anyone here."

Jeremy smiled as he nodded. "Especially where we are, this is a pretty rural spot. There's like a half hour drive into town but there's some good restaurants there."

"Any shopping around here?"

"Oh sure, there's a mall in town."

"What else is there to do?" I grumbled as Porter was shoving more pizza in his mouth.

He shrugged before saying, "We really stay here a lot running the farm. There's a great fishing spot here too. Do you guys fish?"

I laughed harshly before saying, "No. I'm not really the outdoorsy type."

Porter made a strange noise as Jeremy's smile faded. These cowboys might like getting dirty and sweaty outside, but I grew up inside. Air conditioning was my best friend and mud was my enemy. I knew my mom sent me here because she knew I was going to absolutely hate it. But she'd do anything to make me uncomfortable.

"I'll admit I've never fished," Wyatt said as Jeremy turned towards him. "But I'd love to learn. What do you charge for lessons?"

My eyes rolled so hard I was surprised they didn't get stuck in my brain. Since Jeremy wasn't facing me I couldn't see his expression but I could notice a slight blush on his cheeks. "Patience."

"Sign me up."

With another eye roll I stared back at the screen to see the game was still on. When they suddenly showed the cheerleaders my fingers tightened onto my knees. I could feel Wyatt looking at me, knowing he was silently telling me it was okay. My breathing returned to normal when they finally left the screen and the basketball guys came back.

"Would you like me to drive you to see Kurt tomorrow?" Jeremy suddenly asked.

"Sure," I said while finally eating my pizza.

I watched the rest of the game with hardly any interest, honestly sports weren't my thing. Never had been, getting forced by a parent to be on a team in high school really made the appeal go down. The rest of the guys seemed to be invested in the game though. So even though I wanted to be alone, at the same time it was weirdly nice to be around other people. All of the friends I had in high school disowned me when they found out who the real me was. It'd been so long that I've been around people other than Wyatt that it felt weird. Not that Porter and Jeremy were going to become our best friends or anything. But for now, it was nice being around people who weren't judging me. For a moment I felt like a normal guy hanging out with friends. Something people really take for granted.

Once the game was over Porter got up and started grabbing the pizza boxes, bringing them into the kitchen. Jeremy was then turning towards me, his face so soft and nice. That's how a lot of my friends used to look at me, before they knew.

"Want to leave at eight tomorrow? I like to leave a little earlier to grab some coffee."

"Sure, I'm always down for coffee."

"Jeremy does not drink coffee," Porter suddenly said as he walked back into the room. "He drinks sugary iced coffee."

I couldn't help but smile while looking between them. They might have the same face but man, they were pretty different. "There's nothing wrong with that," Jeremy said as he rolled his eyes. "Sorry I don't drink dirt like you do."

Wyatt was now smiling as he looked between them, before looking over at me. I watched as Porter suddenly flicked Jeremy on the forehead before walking up the stairs. Once he was out of sight Jeremy looked back over at me with a twinkle in his eyes. "Let's meet in the kitchen and then we'll go to the hospital."

"Okay."

With that he stood up and stretched, Wyatt's eyes sneakily looking at him. "Well goodnight guys, just holler if you need anything."

He gave a small smile before walking up the stairs and disappearing from sight. "Will you come to the hospital with me?"

"Of course," Wyatt said as he sunk further into the couch. "It'll be nice to see Kurt again."

"Yeah," I said while turning my attention back to the TV. "It will."

*

Walking down the stairs the next morning I yawned before walking into an empty kitchen. My eyes quickly went over to the clock on the oven to see it was exactly eight. I was surprised Jeremy wasn't here yet, or Wyatt for that matter. I shoved my hands into my jean pockets before walking over to the window above the sink, noticing Porter was outside. His dogs were following him, their tails wagging so fast I'm surprised they didn't take off.

His face morphed into a smile as he talked to the dogs before giving their heads a loving pat. He then ran a hand through his thick hair before lifting his tee shirt up to wipe off his face. My face paled when his tan stomach was exposed and god, those abs. I quickly adverted my eyes into the sink while feeling my cheeks heat up stupidly. I only looked up when the door was suddenly opening.

The dogs quickly ran inside and started dancing at Porter's feet. Those green eyes were then looking down at me as he said, "Hey. I'm actually going to be taking you to see Kurt."

"Really?"

With that Wyatt was walking into the kitchen, his eyes looking around the room expectantly. When he obviously didn't see Jeremy he looked at Porter when he started talking. "Jer ate a little too much pizza last night. Cheese can upset him if he eats like a dinosaur, which he did. He ate practically a whole pizza in the middle of the night, then came crawling into my room." He rolled his eyes as he shrugged. "He's a little out of commission today. But let's go."

Wyatt met my eyes as we followed him out of the house and towards a black truck. I snuck into the backseat as they got in, my eyes instantly noticing a cowboy hat on the center console. Country music filled the truck as it drove down the driveway, Porter's eyes finding mine in the rearview mirror.

"You still want coffee?"

"No."

He shrugged before sliding sunglasses over his eyes while pulling out of the farm. My head leaned onto the window as I watched fields and fields roll by. Nothing else seemed to be here, nothing. Wonderful. I don't know how people in the country lived like this. Being on a farm all day seemed so boring and just gross. At least in the city I had things to do. No one to do them with, besides Wyatt, but there were still things to do.

"So uh Wyatt," Porter said as he slowed up for a stoplight. "What did you do in New York?"

"I work in construction."

"Nice."

"What about you Levi?"

It was going to sound stupid when I say I've never really had a real job. Honestly just the odd job here and there because I've always had other things going on. More emotional and mental things going on. But I'm not sure that would be something Porter would understand. "Who says I need to do anything?"

His eyebrows rose up into his shaggy hair but he didn't talk to me the rest of the way to the hospital. We didn't need to talk; I wasn't looking to become best friends with anyone here. Once we were finally at the hospital, we all silently walked inside before Porter led us up a few flights of stairs. After walking down a few more hallways, we were walking into a room where Kurt was lying on a bed. He instantly smiled when he saw us.

"Levi!"

"Hi Kurt," I said while walking towards his outstretched arms.

When he wrapped his arms around me I sighed while completely relaxing into his arms. He's been the only other person besides Wyatt to hug me in a very long time. I did wish he lived closer; he always gave the best hugs and the best advice. My mother didn't like us talking; she always said his progressive thinking corrupted my mind. Which was bullshit.

He hugged me longer before pulling back and placing a hand onto my face. "You look great."

I couldn't help but roll my eyes. "Not quite. How are you? You're looking a little pale."

"Just because I got some medicine earlier," he said with a nonchalant smile. "And seriously, you look good. You're too skinny though. And Wyatt," his smiling face looked over before finding Wyatt. They shared an emotional hug before he said, "You look great too. Any new ink recently?"

Wyatt smiled before taking his jacket off to reveal his tank top. Tattoos covered his entire right arm from his wrist to shoulder, but he also had one on his left pec. He showed Kurt the new tattoo he got before we came out here, the one that completed his sleeve.

"Oh wow," Kurt said as his finger ran over the skin. "That looks great! Thinking of getting any more?"

"Nothings on the horizon for now, but you never know."

Kurt nodded before asking, "How have you been Wyatt? I had no idea you were coming too, I'm so glad you did."

Wyatt shrugged before shoving his hands into his pockets. "Decided to crash Lev's party. And I've been just dandy." When Kurt gave him a look Wyatt sighed before saying, "I've been alright. Honestly just glad to be out of New York for a while."

Just then the door opened and a pretty nurse came in. She looked to be around Kurt's age, with brown eyes and dark hair that was pulled up into a bun. "Hi Porter!" She instantly gave him a hug, his features seeming to soften immediately.

"Hey Debbie," he said after giving her a giant hug.

Debbie was then walking over towards the bed as Kurt said, "Debbie, these are my nephews Levi and Wyatt."

Her face lit up into a smile as she looked between us. "Oh hello! It's so great to meet both of you."

I watched as she walked over to Kurt's bed and started doing nursey things as they quietly talked between each other. My fingers started to sweat as

I looked between her and Wyatt, who was giving me a comforting nod. "Debbie?" Once she turned towards me with a smile I asked, "Would it be okay if I talk to you for a minute? I just need your advice on something medical."

"Oh of course Levi." She must've seen the worried look on my face as she said, "Let's go out into the hallway. We'll be right back," she said while giving Kurt a smile.

Debbie seemed like a nice person and hopefully she wouldn't judge me for my confession. It might be a stretch, but I could only hope.

Three

P orter

    I watched as Levi left the room with Debbie, Wyatt giving him a reassuring smile. It seems like there was something I was missing out on between them. And if he was asking Debbie something I was assuming he was asking her something medical, but what did I know. Kurt got really lucky that she was his nurse because she's probably the nicest woman I've ever met. Since Jeremy and I were constantly coming here she really got to know us. Honestly I consider her part of the family.

"No Jeremy today?"

With a laugh I walked over and hugged him before sinking down into the chair next to his bed. "He ate too much cheese."

He softly laughed as Wyatt took the other seat on the opposite side of the bed. "Well, wouldn't be the first time." He was then looking over at Wyatt as he said, "Reminds me of your mother. She was lactose intolerant but ate cheese and ice cream like mad."

My eyes slid over to Wyatt as I suddenly realized who his mother was. Kurt didn't talk about his family very often, but the stories he's told us were floating back into my mind. I knew he had a sister, Levi's mother, but forgot he had a sister who died. She must be Wyatt's mother. Kurt had been working at the farm forever since he was my dad's best friend. But even though I had known him for so long, he was a pretty private person. It seems that Levi and Wyatt might be the same way.

They started talking between themselves as my phone buzzed in my pocket. I couldn't help but roll my eyes when Jeremy asked to bring home some coffee. He's going to destroy his stomach. After sending him a random gif the door opened and Levi was coming back in. Debbie looked happy like always as she walked back over to Kurt's bed.

We stayed for a while longer before saying our goodbyes and walking back down to my truck. "Jeremy is requesting coffee," I said while sliding into the driver's seat with a huff. "So if anyone wants anything now's the chance."

Wyatt ran a hand over his face while saying, "I'm good."

It only took a few minutes to get to a Starbucks and ordering Jeremy his favorite iced coffee. When I turned around to ask Levi if he wanted anything, I was startled to see him so close. It seemed that he had scooted forward to order, his face quite close to mine. I could see just how long his eyelashes were and the soft curves of his face. He had slight stubble across his jaw that I weirdly wanted to touch.

"Sir?"

The barista's voice snapped me out of the weird trance I was in, clearing my throat while turning towards the screen again. "Do you want anything?" I asked without looking back at him.

"No," he softly said.

"Sorry, that's all."

Once I got the coffee we drove back to the farm in silence, which only made me want to get home faster. After parking I all but fell out of the truck before walking into the farmhouse, noticing Jeremy now on the couch. "Hey," I said while walking over and sitting next to him.

"Thank you so much," he said while grabbing the coffee from my hand. I simply rolled my eyes when he took a giant sip of the drink before setting it onto the coffee table. "How's Kurt?"

"Good," I said while hearing the front door open.

I jumped when fingers were suddenly resting onto mine, making me look up into Jeremy's worried eyes. "You okay?"

With a nod I watched Wyatt walk into the room, Levi following close behind. "Hey Jeremy," Wyatt said with a smile. I saw the instant blush creep onto my brother's cheeks which only made me roll my eyes. The last thing I wanted to witness was my brother flirting with someone, or someone flirting with him. It looks like I'm going to have to have a talk with Wyatt, especially the way he looks at Jeremy. Jeremy hasn't had a boyfriend since high school and that guy turned out to be a dick. The last thing I wanted was for someone else to hurt him like before. The dick from high school had devastated Jeremy so much that he completely gave up on love. No one was going to make him feel like that again.

"Hey," Jeremy said while grabbing his coffee again.

"Feeling better?"

Jeremy nodded while pulling his blanket around his body more. "I am, thanks for asking."

When Levi sat on the other side of Jeremy I got up, making eye contact with Wyatt in the process. "Could we talk outside for a second?"

One of his black eyebrows rose up towards his hair before saying, "Sure."

I knew Jeremy was probably giving me a look but I needed to make sure he was protected. Once we were outside I leaned against the porch while crossing my arms over my chest. Wyatt stood next to me, copying my stance as I dove into my talk.

"Look, I'm not sure what your intentions with my brother are. He's not the kind to have one night stands or hookups. Love is sacred to him and he's been hurt really bad in the past. You might think he's attractive, might want to get into his pants but you're not going to hurt him, not on my watch."

He stayed quiet for a few moments as he looked out into the pastures, where some cows were grazing. His hands then shoved into his pockets as he sighed. "I'm not looking for a one night stand with Jeremy," he softly said before looking back over at me. "I'm not that kind either. I used to be when I was younger but I've been in a bit of a dry spell."

"Okay yeah another thing, I don't want to hear any sex talk between you and Jer. Okay? I think I might puke."

Wyatt chuckled as he ran a hand through his curly hair. "I feel the same way when Levi talks about someone. I know you hardly know me but I promise, I'm not going to hurt him." He gave me a firm look which made me nod.

"Good."

"So... you're okay with me flirting with him?"

With a shrug I said, "As long as you guys don't hump in front of me or anything. But seriously Wyatt," Once shoving my body off the porch I stood right in front of him and looked up into his eyes. "If you hurt him, I'll end you."

"Understood. If you hurt Levi I'll end you."

My cheeks got oddly hot as I stumbled back. "What? Nothing is going on between us."

He simply gave me another look as one of his eyebrows rose. "Whatever you say."

"I'm going to be in the barn if anyone needs me," I grumbled before walking down the porch steps.

Wyatt's words were still making my mind go a million miles a minute. Whatever he thought he saw between us didn't exist. Not because I wasn't attracted to him or anything like that. But people like Levi don't date people like me, we're in completely different worlds. Levi had asked if we had sparkling water, something I've never even muttered in my life. And I wasn't about to try and get close to someone who couldn't be any more opposite than me. Another area Jeremy and I differed was hookups. I had no problem with the random one night stand, maybe that was what I needed. But I needed something to get this weird feeling out of my gut.

Levi

I watched Porter and Wyatt go outside as Jeremy scrolled through the TV channels beside me. "What do you think they're talking about?"

Jeremy briefly looked at the door before shrugging. "No idea honestly. How was the hospital? Sorry I couldn't go with you, my stomach was definitely destroyed."

My eyes landed on the random show he had on as my mind wandered to the conversation with Debbie. She was actually really nice and helped answer a lot of questions I had. "Good, Kurt seemed to be in good spirits."

"I'm glad; it's nice to see him have so many good days. I know he tries to hide it from us when he isn't having a good day." He was then grabbing his coffee and taking a pretty big sip, using the cup to point towards the screen. "Have you ever seen this?"

When I realized he was watching some kind of cooking show I instantly shook my head. "I'm not really into cooking shows, or cooking for that matter."

"No problem, let me change it."

"No, it's okay. You can watch what you want."

His green eyes were then looking at me as he softly smiled. "I don't want to watch something you're not interested in." He was then scrolling through the channels again as he started biting on his straw.

It was still so strange to have someone be nice to me. Since everyone found out why I was different, everyone had shunned me. Wyatt was the only constant thing in my life and also the only person who was nice to me anymore. Jeremy didn't know anything about me, but he seemed like the kind of person to be nice to everyone. There was still doubt in my mind though that he would change when he eventually found out the reason everyone else hated me. But for now I could at least pretend to have a friend.

My body jumped when the door was suddenly opening and Wyatt was once again walking in. He was then sitting on the other side of Jeremy, whose cheeks instantly turned a shade of red. I quickly turned my body sideways so I could meet Wyatt's eyes. When he noticed me staring at him he raised his eyebrows.

"What'd you do with Porter?"

"He's out in the barn." He was then looking at the TV while asking, "What're we watching?"

Jeremy loudly swallowed, his eyes not leaving the screen. "Just scrolling, you can change it if you'd like."

"I'm fine with whatever."

When Jeremy finally settled onto a random show I couldn't help but notice Wyatt completely staring him down. Jeremy was biting on the end of his straw, oblivious to the brown eyes looking at him. Not wanting to watch my best friend hit on someone, I slowly stood up before walking over towards the kitchen. My eyes wandered outside to see Porter talking on his cell phone as he walked towards the barn. He was holding one of those... hmm... what were they called? Saddles, I think. God, this country terminology is not my thing. Anyway, he was holding a saddle against his hip and was now sporting a cowboy hat. He looked like the full on cowboys that were on the front of those cheesy romance books.

As my eyes took in him more, I bit my lip before peeking my head back into the living room. Wyatt and Jeremy were talking about the show that was which only made me frown. Where the fuck was I supposed to go? Against my better judgement I walked outside towards the barn, squinting against the hot sun. God it was so hot and sticky here. This is exactly why I prefer to live inside and not sweat my face off.

Shoving my hands into my pockets I slowly loped into the barn, jumping when I was met with a horse. It was large and staring at me like it wanted to kick me or kill me. Man this horse was gigantic, how do people ride them so easily? Large animals were scary which was why I kept my distance from them.

"Oh, hey Levi."

I jumped from a deep voice behind me, making me basically stumble towards the horse. I gasped and made a high pitched noise as the horse was getting closer to my face, freaking me out more. My body tensed as long arms were suddenly pulling me away from the horse, instantly making me relax. With shaking hands I slowly looked up at Porter's emotionless face, it almost seemed like he was upset.

"Sorry," I whispered as he let go of me and walked over to the horse.

He remained quiet as he swung the saddle onto the horse's back before his green eyes found mine. "Not a horse person?"

"Not really a large animal person." He grunted before turning away. "I mean, I grew up in the city. Not a lot of horses or cows around."

"They won't hurt you," he said a lot softer as he suddenly held his hand out towards me. When I didn't move he grabbed my hand in his larger one, gently pulling me towards the horse. When I tried to back away he put his other arm around me, his fingers still holding mine. "Just relax, they can sense when you're nervous or scared." He was then putting my hand onto the horse's nose, which was still looking at me like it didn't like me. "This is my horse Ace."

I loudly swallowed as my fingers slowly ran over the smooth nose, Porter's fingers still guiding mine. "Hi Ace."

Porter was then sliding his fingers off of mine and stepping back, my body feeling slightly colder. When the horse suddenly sneezed, I squeaked before falling backwards. When I suddenly felt something squish under my foot I hesitantly looked down before gagging.

"Oh my god." I stepped in shit. Literal shit. "Disgusting."

With that Porter sighed before walking back over to Ace. It sounded like he was muttering something but I didn't care anymore. I hated getting dirty and stepping in horse shit was going to make me vomit. Without saying anything else I ran out of the barn and back towards the house. I quickly chucked my shoes off before walking inside, still muttering to myself.

Wyatt looked over at me as I said, "I hate it here. I just stepped in shit!"

I was then running up the stairs and flying into my room. My body was itchy as I jumped into the shower and scrubbed my skin until it turned pink. There's no way I was going to be able to stay here for much longer. But I didn't have much else of an option, unless I wanted to become homeless. My head rested onto the cool tile as the water hit my skin, making me sigh. There was no way I'd go back into that dirty ass barn again.

Four

J eremy

The straw that was headed towards my mouth paused when Levi stormed into the room, looking irate. He yelled about stepping in shit before running up the stairs and slamming the door. I frowned before looking over at Wyatt, who was slowly running a hand over his stubbly jaw. When he sighed he looked over at me before saying, "He's a bit of a clean freak."

"Should I go talk to him?"

He shook his head before saying, "When he gets in moods like this it's better to just leave him alone for a little bit. He'll cool off on his own then he'll be better."

I nodded as he put his left arm on the back of the couch, my eyes suddenly being drawn to his right arm. The swirling ink was catching my eye, his tattoos were very intricate and they looked nice. They disappeared up into the sleeve of his tee shirt but I assumed they went up even higher. When my eyes looked up I felt instant heat in my cheeks when I realized he was already looking at me. Oh god, did he just see me check his arm out?

I busied myself with my drink as I quickly looked away from him and forced myself to look at the TV. "Do you have any tattoos?" He suddenly asked, making me jump as I looked back over at him.

"One," I said with a nervous chuckle. The arm resting behind my body was slowly sliding down the couch, his fingers gently resting against the back of my shirt.

"Really? What is it?"

"Oh uhm," I nervously laughed while my fingers started twiddling with the cup in my hands. "I lost a bet with Porter years ago and the bet was we got to pick a tattoo that the other person would get. When I lost, he got to pick. He kept teasing me telling me he was going to have the guy tattoo something stupid on me, I was so nervous. But luckily he didn't do anything crazy, it's the Sagittarius constellation."

His dark eyebrows rose as he softly smiled. "Really? So a winter baby huh?"

"December first."

His eyes were then roaming over my arms as he asked, "Can I see it?"

My cheeks lit up more as I said, "It's uhm... it's actually on the top end of my ass." Oh my god, how embarrassing!

I watched his eyes slowly travel down my body which only made my breathing pick up even more. When his eyes met mine again I watched him swallow, his Adam's Apple bobbing up and down. His nostrils were flaring ever so slightly before he whispered, "I bet it looks beautiful."

His heated gaze was making me spring up off the couch, almost tripping over the coffee table. "I need to uhm... go help Port!"

With that I all but ran out of the house, gulping in a lot of fresh air. My hands were still shaking as I ran into the barn to see Porter just about to get on Ace. When he saw my flushed face he rose an eyebrow but didn't say anything as I got my horse out. After quickly tacking him up I followed Porter outside where we rode out towards the cows.

We were quiet on the ride out towards the pastures; the peaceful songs of birds making me feel calmer. Once we were in the pasture he suddenly spoke up. "I want to go out tonight."

"Really?"

He nodded, his eyes looking at the cows. "I need to drink or get laid, or both."

"TMI," I said while rolling my eyes.

I never understood how he could always be so open about things so personal. He was fine with talking about who he nailed the previous night. I was a lot shyer than him and was also innocent. Never had sex, never given head or had it done to me. Whereas Porter was bi and had no problem getting a guy or girls attention, I couldn't even get a guy's attention. Well, Wyatt seemed pretty interested in my ass tattoo. I was just really nervous about doing anything sexual at all, it gives me anxiety just thinking about it. Whenever Porter and I went to a bar he always left with someone, and I always left alone. But maybe Levi and Wyatt would want to come this time, at least I'd have someone to talk to.

"I just need a release," he said while running a hand over his face. "Want to come?"

"I'm going to ask Levi and Wyatt if they want to come, is that fine?"

His jaw hardened when I said Levi's name, which was odd. But instead of saying anything bad he said, "Sure, I don't care. As long as I find someone to fuck it'll be good."

"God Porter, you nasty ass."

He gave me a laugh before nodding towards the far end of the field. "Come on, let's ride."

With that he took off in a fast gallop, making me quickly follow him. This was what made me feel alive, feeling the wind hit my face as I flew across the field. Before our dad died he rode with us all the time, which was probably why I liked it so much. He was the reason we were so into the farm and animals. My heart always hurt when I thought of him, I just hope he's proud of me.

*

After our horses were cooled off and tucked away I followed Porter inside to see Wyatt in the kitchen. His dark eyes instantly found mine which only made my stupid cheeks blush. I hated how easily my body reacted to him; it wasn't like I've never seen an attractive man before. But he was dripping in testosterone which only made me weaker. There was something about a manly man that always got me going.

"Want to go to a club tonight?" Porter asked him, Wyatt's eyebrows raising. When he looked at me I dropped my gaze before walking over to grab a water.

"Sure," he slowly said. "I'll tell Levi."

"Let's leave in an hour."

With that Porter left the room, making me slowly look back up into Wyatt's eyes. He leaned against the table before asking, "You club?"

I gave a hard laugh before leaning back against the counter. "No, I honestly can't stand it. I don't really like dancing and I don't drink."

"Then why do you go?"

With a shrug I said, "I don't like being alone. At least I get to hang out with Porter before he hooks up with someone." I hated how pathetic that made me sound. "But you can meet some of the locals, if you're interested." Not really, but maybe they'd like him more than me.

He shook his head before slowly stepping towards me until he was standing right in front of me. His deep voice was then saying, "I won't leave you alone, I promise."

He then left the room, my body falling back against the counter with a sigh. I had no idea how I was going to last when he kept looking at me like that, or talking to me like I was special or something. I took a deep breath before pushing myself off the counter and walking upstairs into my room. I started digging around in my closet, trying to find something decent. Most of my clothes were either work or sleep clothes, not so much going out clothes.

Luckily I had some random clothes stashed in the back of the closet, mainly for emergencies. I opted to go with a fitted black short sleeved button down shirt, dark skinny jeans and of course cowboy boots. I'm sure they didn't go but I didn't feel comfortable in any other kind of shoes. They were pretty scuffed up but they were so worn in they felt like butter. My eyes lingered on the bottle of Giorgio Armani on my dresser that Porter gave me for Christmas. Was cologne overboard? Guess I was about to be overboard. I only squirted a small amount onto my body before shoving my phone into my back pocket.

Once walking out of my room I made a beeline towards Porter's, not bothering to knock before walking in. He was currently sliding a green button down on as I plopped down onto his bed. I watched him walk over to his dresser while rolling his sleeves up before grabbing his watch. His eyes found mine in the mirror as he buttoned his skinny jeans up.

"What's up?"

"Do I look okay?"

He was still putting his watch on as he turned around and looked me over. A smirk was suddenly forming onto his lips as he asked, "Wanting to know if you look good for your brown eyed friend?"

My eyes rolled as he softly chuckled before grabbing his cowboy boots. "Shut up."

"Come on Jer, you look great. You know you don't have to come, I know this isn't really your scene."

With a shrug I said, "I know, but I've been a little cooped up recently. I haven't really been out much. Can you please promise me you'll be careful tonight?"

I watched as he opened up his wallet and pulling a condom out. "I'm always careful, don't worry. Now come on, let's go before the creeps show up."

I followed him down the stairs and saw Levi and Wyatt bickering back and forth between each other. When Wyatt looked over at me he did a double take, making me feel actually good. If he was looking at me like that maybe that did mean I looked somewhat decent.

"Let's drive in two cars," Porter said while grabbing his keys. He was then walking out the front door, making me quickly follow him.

As he was walking towards his truck I realized Wyatt and Levi were following me, not him. Oh man. I tried to calm myself as I slid into my own truck, Wyatt getting into the passenger seat. Oh man. I forced my eyes to not look over at him even though I really wanted to. In the kitchen I briefly saw the tee shirt he was wearing, instantly noticing how it clung to his body. He was also wearing a pair of nice looking jeans and some black shoes. People were going to be flaunting all over him tonight, great.

"So," Levi said as I pulled out of the driveway behind Porter. "Is this a gay club or something?"

"Nah," I said. "Port likes women too; they're who he normally leaves with."

"Oh," Levi quietly said from the backseat. "Has he... been with a lot of women?"

I shrugged while starting to flip through the radio stations. "I don't know, a few. Lately he's been with guys but I'm also not trying to think about my brother's sex life."

He stayed quiet after that as Wyatt asked, "Where exactly is this club?"

"We're going into the city. Cedar Rapids isn't too far but that's where all the action is basically. It'll only take half an hour."

The rest of the quiet was a comfortable silence before I pulled into next to Porter. "The Cactus?" Levi scoffed as I turned the truck off.

With a laugh I looked up at the club with a shrug. "It could have a worse name I guess."

After meeting with Porter, we walked inside the already packed club. Guys and girls were already on the dance floor, music thumping throughout the room. I stayed behind Porter as he walked up towards the bar, the bartender smiling when he saw us.

"Ey, it's the twins! Good to see you guys. Want your usual's?"

"That'd be great, thanks Pat," Porter said as we all sat down at the bar.

I watched Pat place a whiskey in front of Porter, a Coke for me. He'd known us for a while and was a really nice guy. "Hi Pat, these are our friends Wyatt and Levi."

He nodded towards them, giving a smile. "What can I get ya fellas?"

"I'll have a screwdriver," Levi said.

"Just Coke for me," Wyatt said as Pat turned away.

My eyebrows rose as I slowly turned towards him, noticing his chocolate brown eyes were already looking at me. "You're not drinking?"

He gave a soft smile as he shrugged. "I'm fine with not drinking if you're not."

A stupid smile spread across my face as he also smiled, making me notice he has dimples. Oh my god, how have I missed that? He was seriously making me self-conscious, I knew for a fact I wasn't as attractive. Maybe that's why I've never been able to have anyone be interested in me. My smile fell as I turned away from him, Pat putting the drinks onto the bar.

"Hey Porter," a feminine voice suddenly said from behind us. I didn't have to turn around to see who it was, she always found him.

"Hey Julie."

She giggled her little laugh she probably thought was sexy as I finally turned towards her. She was wearing a dress that was barely covering not only her chest but the rest of her private parts. Her long black hair was pulled up into a bun and every time she moved her perfume punched me in the face. When my barstool squeaked her little cat eyes looked over at me with a bored expression.

"Oh. Hey Jeremy."

I wasn't sure why she hated me so much, maybe because I was always around Porter. Good thing the feeling was mutual. "Julie."

She was then turning away as Porter's hands started to slide over her body. "Dance with me?" She breathlessly asked before pulling him out onto the dancefloor.

"Who was that?" Levi asked with disgust.

"One of his normal hookups," I said while staring down at my drink. I didn't need to turn around to know she was grinding all over my brother.

"Glad to know he's into classy people," Levi said before downing his drink.

The three of us stayed in a comfortable silence before Wyatt's left arm was suddenly resting on the back of my barstool. When I didn't move his fingers slowly landed onto my jeans, my entire leg heating up. I didn't look up into his eyes as Levi suddenly got up.

"Going to the bathroom, and then probably dancing. Try to tone down the fun you guys are having."

When he left I downed the rest of my Coke as a slow song suddenly thumped through the club. Goosebumps instantly formed onto my arms when Wyatt suddenly leaned down, his lips close to my ear. "Care to dance?"

My eyes looked over my shoulder out towards the dancefloor, where a lot of people were crammed together. I shook my head while staring down at the bar, my fingers tightening onto my glass. His lips were close to my ear again as he whispered, "Come on, I have an idea."

His strong hand was resting onto the small of my back as he stood up. Since I didn't have anything else to do, I got up and followed him as he led me towards the door. I frowned before looking up at him. "Are we leaving?"

"Not quite," he said with a smile as we walked outside.

He then led me over to the side of the club where people weren't hanging out. The music could still be heard from here, just without all the people. We were even standing under some twinkling lights. This was definitely more my scene. I couldn't help but laugh when he suddenly bowed in front of me, before holding his hands out.

"We're dancing out here?"

"If you're okay with it," he said with a smile. "What do you say?"

I bit my lip while whispering, "Okay." I then grabbed his hand in mine, his other hand resting onto my waist. I smiled while resting my other hand onto his very broad shoulder. He smiled down at me while pulling me a little closer towards his body. "I've actually never danced like this before."

His black eyebrows rose as he asked, "Really? That surprises me."

"Why?"

His fingers slowly ran over my waist as he softly said, "Because you're so attractive. I'm surprised no one has swept you off your feet yet."

My cheeks lit up as I smiled, looking down between us. We continued to sway softly to the music before he leaned down and rested his lips by my ear. He was then softly singing along to the song as I buried my face under his chin. His hand was slowly running up and down my spine, his comforting voice making my eyes close.

Even when the song ended and a thumpy pop song came on, we continued to sway together. As I pulled back I slowly looked up into his eyes, my hand on his shoulder slowly sliding down onto his pec. My fingers curled into his shirt while swallowing nervously. Since I was such a wimp I backed out of his arms while saying,

"I-I'm going to get another drink, and check on Levi."

I then ran back inside and over towards the bar, where Levi was sitting with a frown. He was facing the dancefloor where Julie was grinding her butt over Porter's jeans, his hands on her ass. When she suddenly stood up and started pulling him out of the club, Levi turned back towards the bar.

"I need another drink."

If I drank I'd be drowning myself in alcohol as well but settled for another Coke. Looks like this was going to be a long night.

Five

L^{evi}

My stomach was all in knots as I watched Porter leave with that slut. I mean she was all over him on the dancefloor, but it didn't seem like he cared. Once he left I drank more alcohol until Jeremy gently took the glass from my hand. He was then carefully taking me to his truck, Wyatt lifting me into the vehicle.

My head was pounding, my hands were sweating and my stomach hurt. It'd actually been awhile since I got drunk and this feeling was exactly why. I hated how seeing Porter with that girl made me so upset. I'm pretty sure I annoyed him, since he always seemed to be heavily sighing or staring at me blankly. Why the fuck was I even here? If I wanted to feel like a piece of shit I would've stayed in New York with my mother.

The rocking of the truck was making my stomach feel queasy again as I rested my head onto the seat. When I heard laughter I looked up to see Wyatt and Jeremy smiling between each other. At least someone was having a good night. I wish I would've just stayed at the farmhouse instead of going to that shitty club.

The next thing I knew I was waking up in my bed, a blanket wrapped securely around me. Wyatt was also sleeping next to me, looking pretty peaceful. He must've carried me in when I passed out in the truck. Whoops. With a yawn I ran a hand over my face before carefully getting out of bed. After relieving myself in the bathroom I slowly came out, stopping when I heard voices in the hallway.

"What do you mean?" It sounded like Jeremy.

I pressed my ear against the door to hear someone sigh. Porter's frustrated voice was then saying, "I've never had this problem before. She took me back to her place and... I couldn't get hard. She was even naked and touching herself and nothing! I think my dick is broken."

Jeremy made a noise before softly saying, "Maybe you just need a night off."

"I haven't been laid in weeks! I have been taking a night off."

"Well, maybe it's just Julie."

Porter sighed while saying, "I guess." My ear pressed harder against the door when there was suddenly silence. When I thought they left I suddenly heard, "But how was your night?"

"Good, I actually had fun."

"Awesome, I'm glad. Anyone get drunk?"

Jeremy softly laughed before saying, "Levi was the only one who drank. He passed out in my truck coming home, Wyatt brought him to bed. He wanted to make sure he got through the night alright so he stayed in there with him."

Someone was then yawning, which of course made me yawn. "Go to bed, you look tired. I'll see you in the morning, I'm just going to pop in and check on Levi before turning in."

My eyes widened as I quietly snuck back over to the bed, hitting my shin in the process. I swallowed my scream before sinking down onto the bed, pulling the blanket up around me. Wyatt groaned next to me right as the door ever so slowly opened. My heart was beating out of control as I tightly shut my eyes and forced myself to slow my breathing.

I heard footsteps slowly walk over towards the bed before seeming to stop in front of me. Fingers were then gently running through my hair, which actually felt really nice. I'd always loved when people touched or played with my hair. His fingers were then leaving my hair, but his footsteps didn't move and I could sense he was still in front of me.

After a few more silent moments he finally walked towards the door, before it gently closed it a moment later. Once he was gone my eyes opened as I flopped onto my back. My heart was still beating like crazy, knowing Porter had just touched me. Why was he even checking on me? Did he think I was poor with liquor? Little did he know that I actually wanted to get drunk. How the fuck was I supposed to fall asleep now?

*

I slept like shit that night, hardly getting a few hours. Once the sun came up I sleepily got up and wandered into the bathroom. After my business was done I carefully walked down the stairs, walking towards the kitchen. I stopped in my tracks when I saw who I thought was Porter at the stove, before realizing it was Jeremy when he turned around. He smiled while doing something with the bacon on the stove.

"Morning Levi. Want any coffee?"

"That'd be great." My tired body practically fell down into a chair as he handed me a large cup. "Thank you."

"No problem."

I watched him finish up the food he was making before setting it onto the table. There was bacon, scrambled eggs and biscuits. My eyebrows rose as I watched him turn the oven off, wiping his hands off onto a towel. "Wow, you went all out."

He softly smiled while giving a small shrug. "I was up early anyway doing chores." He was then piling eggs and bacon onto a biscuit before grabbing a worn out baseball hat and putting it backwards onto his head. "I'll be fishing if uhm... Porter is wondering."

After giving me a small nod before leaving the room as my eyes wandered down to the food. I grabbed a biscuit and started nibbling on it as Wyatt was suddenly walking into the kitchen, his eyes wandering around the room expectantly. When he saw only me he sat down, eyeing the food and basically drooling.

"How're you feeling?"

"Fine," I mumbled as he started nibbling on the bacon.

"Where'd all this food come from?"

I watched him then build the same kind of sandwich Jeremy did. "Jeremy made it, he went out fishing."

Wyatt's black eyebrows rose up into his hair. "Really?"

"Okay, what's up with you two? Did something happen between you guys last night?" When he shook his head I frowned, leaning my head onto my hand. "Not even a kiss?"

"We slow danced outside the club." His face was then turning all sappy as he smiled down at the table. "It was one of the best nights I've ever had. Then you had to get drunk and the night ended early."

After rolling my eyes he slowly stood up. "How was I supposed to know you were going to make a move? Ugh, my head is starting to pound. I'm going to go take a nap."

"Didn't you just get up?"

He chuckled when I glared at him while standing up. "Shut up."

"I'll be outside if you need me, but try not to need me."

"Let me guess, you're going to go fish?"

"As a matter of fact yes. So please go to Porter if you need anything."

My face weirdly lit up as he grabbed more food and left, the room feeling very lonely. I stared down at the rest of the coffee in my mug before dumping it down the drain. My stomach was all up in knots as I slowly climbed the stairs and wandered back into my room. Once I fell onto the bed I yawned, turning the TV to a random show. It wasn't too much longer that my eyes were closing and I was sucked back into the darkness.

Wyatt

I ran a hand through my shaggy hair while trying to figure out where someone would fish around here. Fishing was something I've never done but I'd love to learn, especially if Jeremy was the teacher. Ever since I first saw him I knew I wanted him. Not just for his body, which was honestly like a work of art, but for the person he was. I loved when he smiled and his green eyes crinkled or when he stared at my tattoos. I'd love more than anything to feel his fingers on my skin and to kiss those amazing lips. Holding him in my arms last night was amazing and only wished it lasted longer. His body molded perfectly against mine like it was meant to always be there. I'd never wanted anyone as much as I wanted Jeremy, and wish I could make him want me too.

After walking around the backside of the farm, I noticed a lake in the distance and a pier where Jeremy was sitting. I shoved my hands into my pockets before walking over; noticing pop music was playing from a small speaker behind him. He was holding a fishing pole but what made my mouth water the most was the fact he was shirtless. His creamy skin looked delectable in the sun and only made my fingers itch to touch him. He was wearing a baseball hat backwards onto his head, his brown hair clinging to his neck. If only his shorts were riding even lower to reveal the tattoo I desperately wanted to see.

"Hey Jeremy."

He immediately jumped and almost dropped his fishing pole into the water before recovering. Once he was facing me I noticed he had sunglasses on, making me wish I could look into those amazing eyes.

"Hi Wyatt." Another thing I loved was my name on his lips.

"Mind if I join you?"

When he remained silent one of my eyebrows rose before he seemed to snap out of his trance. "O-of course. Sorry, I only have one fishing rod."

"Not a problem," I said while sitting down next to him with a smile. A soft breeze was shoving my hair around as I tried not to ogle him too much. "So," I said after clearing my throat. "Just how hard is it to learn how to fish?"

My heart started beating faster when he turned towards me with a smile. "Not too hard, you just need an open mind."

"Good thing my mind is very open. Would you be okay with teaching me? I don't want to disturb your alone time."

He shook his head before pulling the line out of the water and handing the rod over to me. He was then turning towards me, one leg hiked up underneath him as his other leg skimmed the water. "Okay, so first I'm just going to explain the basics."

I watched as his fingers ran over everything he was talking about, showing me what I needed to know. I really had no idea what anything was but loved hearing him explain everything to me. "Now this is how you cast a line." I watched him effortlessly cast a line out perfectly before showing me what to do if I caught a fish. Like I'd actually be catching anything. "That should be everything for now. Any questions?"

With that he handed the rod back to me, another smile on his face. "Just one," I whispered before leaning forward until our faces were closer. His body slightly tensed before he bit his bottom lip, which only made me weaker. "Can I take your sunglasses off?"

He stayed silent for a few moments before slowly nodding. My free hand was then gently sliding them off his face, those green eyes finally coming into sight. His cheeks were also slightly pink and man, what a sight to see. "Uhm, why did you want my sunglasses off?"

"Because I wanted to see your eyes."

His cheeks lit up more as he softly smiled before looking out at the water. "I don't know why, they aren't interesting."

"Hey," I said while gently putting my fingers onto his chin. When he looked back at me I said, "Everything about you is interesting."

My thumb ran over his soft skin as he smiled before looking back down at the water. Even though I wanted to keep touching him, I dropped my hand and forced myself to calm down. Since he was still looking at the water I glanced around, noticing a bottle of sunscreen behind him.

"Mind if I use some?"

Once he looked at the bottle he shook his head. "Go for it."

He offered to hold the fishing pole as I slowly slid my shirt off, dropping it onto the pier behind me. I smiled when he looked over at me before quickly looking away. I was then lathering up my arms and chest before holding it out to him, deciding to take a chance. "Mind getting my back?"

Those green eyes turned towards me, his cheeks lit up like a Christmas tree. "Oh uhm, sure."

After handing the pole back to me, I watched him get up and move behind my body. Once his fingers were running over my shoulders, I couldn't help the groan that slipped out of my mouth. His fingers hesitated for a few moments before continuing down my back. I needed to think of a conversation topic before I scared him off.

"So I was wondering," I said as his fingers moved over my spine, making me shiver. "Do you just not like the taste of alcohol or have you ever had a drink?"

He remained silent for a moment before he sighed, his fingers tightening on my back. "My mom's an alcoholic. She also got into drugs and I... I was afraid of ending up like her. I have a slightly addictive personality and was afraid I'd be exactly like her."

His fingers completely stopped moving as he sighed, making me frown. "I'm sorry for bringing up any bad memories."

"No, you're fine. You were just asking."

When he sat down next to me I looked over at him while asking, "I take it you guys aren't close?"

"That's one way to put it," he said with a frown. "We've never really been close. Our parents divorced when we were little and our dad had primary custody. Our dad was a lot closer to us than she was, but he actually paid attention to us. When Porter and I came out to her, she was livid. She tried to hit me but Porter grabbed me and took me home. When our dad found out she tried to hit me, he got sole custody of us. I haven't seen her in years honestly; she didn't even come to my dad's funeral."

"God Jeremy, I'm so sorry."

He sadly smiled before shrugging. "I've learned to live with it. It would've been nice to have a mom growing up but there are people who have it worse."

I then wrapped my arm around him and pulled him into my side, his head sliding under my jaw. "Doesn't mean what you went through wasn't awful."

"What about you?" He suddenly asked as his fingers softly landed onto my stomach. "Are you close with your parents?"

"My mom was killed by a drunk driver when I was ten and I never knew who my father was."

He pulled back, his face so sad. "I'm so sorry Wyatt. It's like we're a couple of misfits."

"If you're a misfit I'd love to be considered one too."

His smile grew before he started biting his bottom lip, my eyes looking down at his lips. When I slowly started leaning towards him my heart started beating faster when he wasn't pulling away. The fishing pole in my hand suddenly started moving, making Jeremy instantly look over.

"Oh my god, you have a bite!" He was then helping to reel the tiny fish in, his face looking like a proud parent. "You got one!"

My eyes traveled down the squirming fish in his hands. Who knew a fish could be a cock block. But the look of pure happiness on Jeremy's face was making a smile form onto my face. I watched as he started rummaging around in his shirt before bringing up his phone.

"It's mandatory that you get your picture taken with the first fish you catch." I couldn't help but laugh as he held his phone up. "Smile big!"

After the picture he showed me how to release it, before he was gently putting it back into the water. "You're a really good teacher," I said while nudging his shoulder with mine.

His cheeks lit up as he started biting his bottom lip, which was honestly so damn sexy. "It was all you." Those green eyes were then looking up at me before he softly asked, "Do you have your phone on you?" With a nod I grabbed it out of my pocket and held it out, watching as he grabbed it. "Thanks."

Before I could ask why he wanted it a wicked smile came across his face as he pushed me off the pier. Once I swam up to the surface I spit some water out, looking up at his laughing face. "It's like that huh?" I asked with a smile.

His body was lightly shaking with laughter as I grabbed the side of the pier and hoisted myself up. He was watching me intently as I slowly crawled over to him, water dropping from my hair falling onto his leg. I swallowed loudly while slowly taking his hat off and placing it on the pier behind him. Right as I was about to throw him in, I was stunned when his hand reached up and touched my wet curls. I fucking loved when people touched my hair and having him run those slender fingers through it made it even better. The hand in my hair slowly ran down until it was on my cheek, making me close my eyes and swallow hard. The next thing I knew I was falling back into the water.

When I came up the second time, Jeremy was laughing his ass off and basically crying. "Oh it's on now," I said while climbing out.

He squeaked and got up, laughing as he started to run away. My long legs instantly caught up with him before my arms wrapped around his waist, his laugh so contagious. His fingers were gripping onto my arms but he wasn't trying to pry me off as we walked closer to the water.

"You're so sneaky," I whispered in his ear as we got to the end of the pier. He was still laughing so hard, his breathing coming out in little pants.

Before he could respond I gently threw him into the water. When he came up for air he was still laughing as I reached down to help him up. We ended back on the end of the pier, legs dangling over the sides. I wanted to kiss or touch him but didn't want to make him feel uncomfortable. And right now he looked so free and breezy; I really wanted him to stay like that.

"Well that was a nice refreshing break," I said as he giggled.

"I would apologize but it was pretty funny. Come on! Let's see who can get the most fish."

With that he put his baseball hat back onto his head as he handed me the fishing line. He then started diving into stories from his childhood and all the good memories he had fishing with Porter and his dad. We definitely started to have a moment earlier but I think for now it passed. Which was fine, I'd just have to be patient. And Jeremy is definitely someone I will wait for. Even if it took forever, I'd wait. Because as I looked at his smiling face, I knew there was no way I could go back to New York now. My heart was already in the country. Now if only I could get this shy cowboy to open up to me.

Six

P orter

    I just finished putting the rest of the food onto the table when Jeremy and Wyatt walked into the kitchen. They were both laughing and seemed to be in really high spirits, which made me really happy. It'd been such a long time since I had seen my brother with an actual smile on his face; it was so refreshing to see. If Wyatt could make him this happy, I'd gladly want him to stay. It might take longer for him to open his heart up, but I really hoped he did.

"Hey," I said as they sat down at the table. "How was fishing?"

"Wyatt caught three fish!"

"Nice going city boy."

He rolled his eyes with a laugh. "Thanks country boy. Speaking of city boy, is Levi down here?"

"Not that I know of," I said as Jeremy started digging into the food.

If one of us made breakfast or lunch, we agreed the other one would make the next meal. It had started when we were younger and couldn't agree on who would cook. Thank god our dad taught us everything we needed to know about cooking or else we'd be fucked.

"I'll go get him," Wyatt said as he started to get up.

"I'll go, it's fine."

With that I walked out of the kitchen but slowly turned around when I was far enough away. When I looked back into the kitchen I saw Jeremy telling some story, Wyatt staring at him with a look that seemed very intimate. It was pretty obvious Jeremy didn't realize how Wyatt was looking at him, like they were the only people around.

I quickly turned around and walked up the stairs while feeling a weird ping in my chest. I was happy Jeremy was happy, ecstatic. I would be lying if I said I wasn't jealous of that. Having someone look at me like that or even having someone to talk to like that. My entire adult life had basically been hook ups and one night stands that it was all I knew. Trying to hook up with Julie had changed my mind on certain things, or maybe I was still shook up that my dick didn't get hard. Maybe it was trying to tell me something, like to make a change. Or maybe I was a fucking idiot who was talking to his dick.

With a scowl I ran a hand over my face before softly knocking onto Levi's door. "Levi?"

After a few seconds the door slowly opened where a disheveled Levi looked up at me. My throat felt weirdly dry as I stared down at his slender face, suddenly getting the urge to touch his skin. What is wrong with me? There's no way we could ever end up together, we're too opposite. Fuck that opposites attract saying.

"There's lunch downstairs if you're hungry."

"Okay," he softly said before opening the door more. I frowned when I saw the dark bags under his eyes, his disheveled hair and pale skin.

"Are you okay?"

"I'm fine."

I frowned more when I placed a hand onto his forehead. "You're burning up."

"I'm really okay."

After I gave him a flat look he sighed, leaning his body more onto the door. "Get back into bed." When he didn't move I crossed my arms over my chest, raising an eyebrow. "Levi, you need to get back into bed."

He grumbled but eventually did wander back into bed, his movements very slow. Once he was pulling a blanket over himself I walked into the bathroom, grabbing a washcloth. After it was damp I walked back over to him before sitting on the side of the bed. I ran a hand over his slightly sweaty forehead to move his blonde hair out of his eyes. I then gently placed the washcloth onto his skin.

"I said I was okay," he whispered as his eyes closed for a moment before sleepily opening again. "Seriously Porter, don't worry about me."

My free hand ended up onto his cheek, my thumb slowly running over his cheek. "Well Levi, you're just going to have to accept that someone is going to take care of you." His cheeks lit up, the warmth under my hand making me clear my throat before pulling my hands away. "I'm going to go grab you some crackers and something to drink. Do you want anything else?" When he shook his head I stood up while saying, "I'll be right back."

I was then quickly walking down the stairs before ending up in the kitchen again, Wyatt and Jeremy still laughing with each other. Wyatt's dark eyes looked behind me before finding my eyes. "Is Levi coming down?"

"He's actually not feeling great."

Wyatt frowned, his face twisting with worry. "Really? I'll go bring him-"

"That's okay," I said while reaching into the pantry and grabbing a box of crackers. "I'm going back up. Jer, do you mind doing my chores tonight in the barn?"

"Of course," he said as I grabbed some water and a Gatorade.

With a nod I walked back upstairs, knocking softly on Levi's door. Those tired eyes looked over at me and watched me the entire time I walked over towards his bed. When I placed the items on the table he rolled his eyes. "I told you I was fine."

He then started coughing before resting onto his side and burying his face into the pillow. When I raised an eyebrow at him he simply said, "Shut up."

I chuckled before repositioning his washcloth and pulling the blanket further up his body. "Do you need anything right now?"

He shook his head before sniffling. "Don't stay Porter; I'll just get you sick."

"That's a chance I'm willing to take."

Another coughing fit was taking over him before he looked up at me with tired eyes. "No Porter, you shouldn't get sick. You have all the cows and horses."

I couldn't help but smile at the concern in his voice. "That's why I have a brother." When his fingers were suddenly tightening on the pillow I softly asked, "What's wrong?"

"My stomach hurts," he whispered as he tightly shut his eyes. "Porter, I think I'm going to throw up."

When he whimpered I scooped him up in my arms and brought him into the bathroom. After positioning him in front of the toilet I gently rubbed his back as he threw up. Once he was done I flushed the toilet, wiping his mouth off with a fresh rag.

"I'm sorry," he whispered as his fingers tightly gripped onto my arms.

"Why are you sorry?"

"For being sick."

His face was then twisting up again before throwing up more. I made sure to clean him up again after flushing. "You have no reason to apologize Levi, everyone gets sick."

Once he wanted to lie down again I carefully picked him up and made sure to get him comfortable again. I then gave him medicine for his nausea and handed him some Gatorade to sip on. "Thank you," he whispered as his eyes slowly closed. When his breathing got heavier I slowly stood up which made his eyes snap open. "Are you leaving?"

I couldn't help but smile, seeing as how not too long ago he was telling me to not stay. "I can stay if you want; I was going to let you get some rest." The look on his face was making me sit back down. "I'll stay. Want me to turn a movie on?"

He slowly nodded, making me get up and turn his TV on. After finding Jurassic Park I smiled, making sure to turn the volume down. "Fucking love this movie," I said while walking back over to the bed.

I noticed he was softly smiling while those big blue eyes looked up at me. "You love dinosaurs?"

"Hell yeah I do, you don't?"

"No, I do." He was then scooting over and gently patting the bed, his face still really pale. "Come watch it."

I swallowed hard while getting up onto the bed. "Tell me if you need to go back into the bathroom okay? Or if you need anything."

With a nod his eyes closed, his face burying into the pillow. I took the washcloth on his forehead and gently patted his skin with it before removing the rag. My gaze lingered on him for a few moments longer, his breath slowing down as he drifted off to sleep. My fingers then gently touched his cheek, feeling myself smile. I forced myself to turn my attention to the movie and take my hands off of him. I wasn't sure why my body was reacting to his so much but there was no way I was leaving him. I settled in to watch the movie, resting my head against the headboard. All I knew was I hadn't felt so drawn to a person in a long time... if ever. This city boy was starting to melt my cold country heart.

Levi

Everything felt like shit as my eyes slowly opened, trying to swallow down the nausea. After blinking a few times I looked up and saw Porter still sitting next to me, weirdly making my stomach flutter. My eyes wandered over his tan face and his shaggy brown hair. His jawline was pretty spectacular and only made me more envious. I then looked down his strong arms and his thick legs, down to his bare feet. I then looked towards the TV to see Jurassic Park still playing, what looked like the end.

When I looked up my cheeks instantly got hot when those dark eyes were looking down at me. The sudden eruption of butterflies in my stomach made me also feel like throwing up. It must've been obvious on my face because he quickly picked me up and brought me back into the bathroom. I threw up everything in my stomach before pulling back and breathing heavily. When Porter helped cleaned me up and flushed the toilet, more butterflies appeared in my stomach. He then helped me stand up, before I greedily grabbed my toothbrush and cleaned out my mouth.

My eyes caught my reflection making me frown, my toothbrush dangling in my mouth. My face was pale and gross, my eyes bloodshot and my hair sticking up in random places. I looked absolutely disgusting and also felt like shit. I hadn't felt this shitty in a long time. I simply continued brushing my teeth, at least feeling a little better. When I continued to stare at my reflection with a frown I jumped when a hand landed onto my back.

I looked up to look into his eyes looking at me with worry. "You okay?"

"Yeah," I whispered before he picked me back up and carried me to bed.

When he tucked me in and climbed on top of the blanket besides me, I couldn't stop thinking about how strange this was. Porter was still basically a stranger to me, I knew nothing about him. He didn't know anything about me, which was good. Because once he learned the truth he'd never talk to me again. And I really wasn't ready for that.

"Porter?" I whispered, his eyes instantly turning towards me. "Can I have a sip of a drink?"

He nodded; grabbing the Gatorade and helping me sit up so I could drink. Once I was done I slowly lowered my body back onto the bed, my eyes feeling very heavy. "Do you want to try a cracker?" He suddenly whispered, making me look up at him before nodding.

I watched him grab a saltine before holding it up to my lips, my stupid cheeks feeling really hot. After taking a small bite I watched as his thumb slowly ran over the corner of my mouth, where I'm sure crumbs were. He was also staring at me with a look I hadn't seen before on him, and had no idea what it meant. That look quickly vanished, so fast that I thought I had imagined it. Instead of trying to decipher it I lowered my head back down and closed my eyes. Before I knew it I was slipping back into a deep sleep.

When my eyes opened later the room was dark and quiet. I could instantly feel Porter's body heat next to me before I even looked up at him. From the sound of his breathing it seemed he was asleep, which felt weirdly intimate to me. It was nice being next to someone in bed and listen to their even breathing. It was so personal and real, something I've really craved.

After rubbing my eyes I slowly looked up and couldn't stop the smile from forming on my face. He was still sitting against the headboard, his arms lightly crossed over his chest. That dark hair of his was hanging slightly down in his closed eyes, making me want to push it off his forehead. My eyes traveled down his body to see his shirt riding up a little on his arm, making tattoos on his bicep come into view. They seemed to be roman numerals, not sure what they meant. But I'd love to run my fingers over them, tattoos were hot as fuck.

Luckily my stomach was feeling a little better so sitting up didn't make me feel like puking. The Gatorade bottle was sitting next to Porter's body, making me slightly frown. After taking a slight peek up at his still sleeping face, I slowly leaned across his body. My body was pretty close to his, having to bite my bottom lip so I wouldn't accidentally make a weird ass noise. This was a pretty unfortunate time to have such short arms but luckily I was able to grab the bottle. When I pulled the bottle closer to my body, a hand was suddenly landing onto the small of my back.

With a squeak I jumped and dropped the bottle, gasping when realizing I dropped it onto Porter's crotch. Kill me now. "Oh my god," I said when he winced and held his pants. "I'm so sorry," I said while holding the bottle against my chest before looking up into his eyes.

He was sleepily smiling, making me realize his hand was still on me. His fingers were slowly running over my shirt as he said, "Don't worry about it darlin'. I don't want kids anyway."

My entire face lit up with a blush as his eyes closed again, his breathing becoming heavy. Did he seriously call me darlin'? What the fuck was that about? The amount of butterflies in my stomach was making me actually feel nauseous. I all but fell off the bed while running into the bathroom and basically fell down in front of the toilet. When nothing came up except stupid dry heaves, I frowned before swallowing heavily. Okay Levi calm down... he was obviously talking in his sleep. He didn't mean to call me that, and it isn't like he'd ever call me that again.

After my stomach settled down I walked back out into the room, Porter's sleeping body now slouched over the bed. His head was resting on the pillow I had been using; his hands under his face making him look adorable. Even though I wanted to go back into bed, I slowly wandered out the room and down the stairs.

I followed the sound of a TV into the living room to see Jeremy and Wyatt watching a movie on the couch. Jeremy was currently laughing at something an actor said but it was the way Wyatt was looking at him that made my eyebrows raise. I obviously knew he had the hots for Jeremy, but wasn't sure if he had acted on those feelings yet. From the way he was staring at him he wanted to, but Jeremy must be more reserved about it. I really admired Wyatt in that sense; he never pushed anyone into anything. He's a great man and I always felt lucky he was family.

His eyes instantly wandered over to me as I walked into the room. "Hey," he said. "Feeling any better?"

With a nod I walked over and plopped down into a large armchair. "A little yeah. Not sure why I'm feeling like shit."

"Maybe it's one of those twenty four hour bugs?" Jeremy softly asked as his eyes seemed to get heavy.

"I hope so," I said with a sigh. "Being sick is fucking annoying."

"Do you need anything?" Wyatt suddenly asked as he stood up. "I'm going to go grab a drink, you want one?"

"Maybe some water." With a nod he left and quickly came back, handing me a cup of cold water. I held it up against my head which actually helped. "Could I ask you something Jeremy?"

His gentle eyes were looking over at me as he smiled. "Of course."

"Does Porter usually call people darlin'?"

His dark eyebrows rose as he tucked his legs up under his body on the couch. "He only calls people he cares about a nickname."

It was my turn to blush while spitting out, "Wait, what? People he cares about?"

Jeremy nodded while leaning into the back of the touch. "I've only heard him call one other person a nickname before. When we were in high school he was dating this girl who he absolutely loved. He called her sweetheart, and that's the only other person he's said something like that to."

I swallowed loudly, my stomach twisting in knots. "What happened?"

Jeremy frowned before saying, "She cheated on him. It absolutely destroyed him and since then he only has hooks ups and random one night stands."

"Somebody actually cheated on him?"

He nodded, a frown forming onto his face. "She was a bitch. She actually married Porter's best friend, who she cheated on him with. They moved somewhere on the east coast."

I frowned while placing my hands onto my stomach again. "I need to go lay back down." Before anyone could say anything else I quickly walked back up the steps and back into my room.

My eyes lingered on Porter still sleeping on the bed, still not believing his girlfriend would cheat on him. With his best friend of all people. With a shaky breath I walked over to the bed, quickly realizing there wasn't any room for me to lay down. His giant body was making the bed look tiny, but he was looking too comfortable to wake up. Once I sat down onto the side of the bed his dark eyes were suddenly opening and quickly finding mine.

He rubbed his eyes while yawning before slowly sitting up. "Shit, did I fall asleep?" His voice was so deep it made goosebumps form onto my arms.

"It's okay," I softly said.

"Sorry Lev, didn't mean to pass out. How are you feeling?"

When he moved over a little I slowly lowered my body down, heavily sighing as my face lowered into the pillow. "Better."

"That's good."

He was smiling sweetly at me while pulling a blanket up over my body. "What do your tattoos mean?"

His eyes briefly glanced down at his skin before finding my eyes again. "It's my dad and Kurt's birthday, the most important men in my life."

"What happened to your dad?" When he frowned I felt like shit, hoping I wasn't bringing up any bad memories. "Sorry if that wasn't appropriate-"

"It's okay," he said while leaning his head against the headboard. "He had a heart attack."

"I'm so sorry."

His eyes seemed to glaze over as he stared at the wall. "He was my role model and biggest inspiration. We had no idea he was going to be taken so early from us." When he got silent I rested a hand onto his arm, his eyes looking down at me. He softly smiled before resting his hand on top of mine. "Kurt was best friends with my dad and they'd been working together on the farm forever. Since my mom is an alcoholic piece of shit, Kurt took care of us when our dad died."

"I can relate to the shitty mom part, I'm sorry you had to go through that."

"Thanks Lev." I really liked when he called me that, especially when he said that nickname and smiled.

Instead of saying anything else his body slowly lowered back down onto the bed. He was still on top of the blankets but this still felt so... intimate. The way he was looking at me made me think of the darlin' comment from earlier, and if I should bring it up. But he probably wouldn't remember it anyway; he had to have been asleep.

"Try to get some sleep," he whispered as my eyes shut.

I should probably tell him something personal since he told me about his parents, but I was scared. Because once I got more personal with him moments like these wouldn't be happening anymore. And I wasn't sure if I was ready for that quite yet.

Seven

J eremy

I ran a hand through my sweaty hair while walking back into the house.
After grabbing some water I walked up the stairs but stopped when I heard
Wyatt's voice coming from Levi's room. Normally I wouldn't eavesdrop
but their conversation made me stop in the hallway.

"I still don't get why you don't want me to come," Levi's voice was saying.

"Don't worry Levi, you'll be fine here. But I can't put off going to New
York any longer, especially for this."

Since I felt wrong for listening, I quickly wandered into my room before
taking a long and hot shower. Once out I walked out into the hallway and
almost ran into Wyatt. "Oh hey," he said with a smile. "I was looking for
you."

I forced my stomach to stop getting butterflies while looking up at him. I
knew most people didn't have a problem getting close to someone else, but
I did. For the most part I didn't feel like I deserved the attention, all because
of someone from the past. It's crazy how people can mess you up and make
you feel like you aren't worthy of anyone.

And honestly, Wyatt could be a model. What would someone like him want to stay in Iowa for? New York would have more opportunities for him anyway, and better guys there. But every now and then he would look at me a certain way and I'd wonder what he would possibly want with someone like me. He could have anyone he wanted, why was I so special? Because I never felt that way.

"What's up?"

"I actually need to go to New York this weekend, to clear up some business ties. Would you be interested in taking a little trip?"

"You want me to go with you?"

He nodded while shoving his hands into his pockets. "Have you ever been to New York? I thought it might be a fun road trip for you if you've never been."

"I've never been no, but would I just be in the way? I don't want to be a bother if you're going for business reasons."

Wyatt simply gave me a look before saying, "You'd never be a bother Jeremy."

The soft way he said that made my stomach twist up in knots as I stared at his face. I honestly had no idea why he had been so nice to me since he came to the farm. I was nothing special but being around him was starting to make me feel like I was, like I was worthy of the attention. And maybe just a weekend wouldn't be so bad; it would be a little scary traveling without Porter though. We'd been together literally our whole lives, never been separated. That was one of the reasons why I felt so comfortable here, because I was safe. And having someone else who made me feel safe would be so strange. Hopefully if I were to allow myself to fall for him, he wouldn't just end up leaving in the end.

Without giving it another thought I swallowed my fear and said, "Okay."

He immediately smiled before saying, "Great! I may know some good tourist spots too."

I laughed before starting to think about walking around New York with him. Grabbing some food and taking in the sights... I had to stop day-dreaming before I lost my mind. "I'm just ah... going to go and uh... tell Porter."

Before he could respond I ran away before I could get sucked into his eyes and smile. Why the hell did I say yes to going across the country with him? I barely know him. Not that I thought he would just take me there to murder me but still, I didn't know him at all. He didn't even know that I had basically no experience in the dating world or... god. He probably wasn't even thinking about dating me yet here I was overthinking literally everything. Hopefully he wouldn't regret taking me.

Since I was still overthinking as I ran into the barn, I almost lost my footing while rounding the corner. Luckily my body slid into a hay bale instead and I didn't go slamming into the concrete. When I looked up I realized Porter was staring at me with one eyebrow raised, a bag of grain hoisted up onto his shoulder.

"Where's the fire?" His deep lazy voice asked as he walked towards the grain room.

"So uhm," I said while twisting my fingers together. "I'm going to New York with Wyatt. This weekend."

His eyebrows rose as he glanced over at me. "Are you coming back?"

"Well yeah, of course. Why wouldn't I?"

He shrugged before saying, "The way you're freaking out you're acting like you guys are going to get hitched and move there."

"Wh... hitched? You're nuts Port."

"Yeah, and so are you Jer. It sounds like you guys are going on a trip, why are you freaking out so much?"

When he left the room I quickly followed him like a lost puppy. "Maybe because I hardly know the man."

Porter gave me a look as he picked up a bag of grain and started to walk away again. "Okay so if you're that nervous about going, don't."

"Well I mean, I kind of want to go."

He laughed as he put the bag down and gave me a hard look. "Then what's the problem? Why are you acting so crazy?"

My fingers started ringing together as I said, "We've never been apart."

His face softened as he leaned against the wall. "Is that what this is about? I swear Jeremy you overthink more than anyone I know."

"Thanks for the boost of confidence."

"It's not like you're not coming back because I wouldn't be okay with that. I do want you to go and experience things outside of the ranch. I think it'll be good for you."

I rolled my eyes while sitting down onto a hay bale. "You're making it seem like I'm a five year old. And what about you, you don't want to go experience things?"

His eyes glanced over towards where the house was before shrugging. "I've had plenty of experiences and let's be honest, I've had more than you. I want you to go live and Wyatt is a good guy to go with, he'll know his way around New York. I'm perfectly content staying here." When I stayed silent he asked, "What else is making you nervous?"

"It's just... he's making me scared. I've been feeling myself almost start to fall for him."

"It's okay to open yourself back up to someone, especially someone who obviously likes you. Just don't let yourself overthink like you always do and have a good time. Eat a lot of good food for me okay?"

That made me laugh and finally relax my fingers. "You know I will. You don't think he would... try anything on me do you?"

His face got serious again as he said, "If he does I'll kick his ass. If he tries anything that you don't want I'll come pick you up myself."

That made me get up and wrap my arms around him, his strong arms wrapping around me too. "Sorry I always overreact and freak out."

His chest shook with laughter as he said, "It's just one of the things I love about you. It'll be okay Jeremy; it's going to be a fun weekend." He then pulled back before saying, "But help me with chores first."

"Fine, fine."

With that he shoved the grain bag into my arms as we walked into the barn. I couldn't stop my mind from running, thinking of all the different scenarios the weekend might hold. There's definitely nothing scary about going across the country with someone my heart desperately wanted... psh. Not at all.

Eight

L^{evi}

"You sure you guys have everything?" I asked while looking between Wyatt and Jeremy. Jeremy had been nervously fidgeting since he woke up, Porter doing his best to calm him down. I wasn't quite sure why Jeremy seemed to be so riled up, but luckily Porter got him an iced coffee which seemed to help.

Even though they were only going to be gone for a weekend, I was still sad. I really hadn't been away from Wyatt... well ever. I was nervous about being alone here on the farm with Porter for the weekend.

"I'm pretty sure," Jeremy said while looking another look around at his bags.

"If we forgot anything we can always swing by a store once we get there," Wyatt said with a smile.

That seemed to calm Jeremy down as he nodded before digging around in a bag. The way that Wyatt was watching him made me advert my eyes from their moment and looked over at Porter. He was leaning against the porch watching them before his eyes glanced over at me. My breath hitched before quickly turning away as Jeremy walked over towards his brother. I could see them hugging as Wyatt smiled down at me and also hugged me.

"Call me if you need anything," his deep voice said in my ear as he squeezed my body.

"You're going to be across the country."

He laughed before saying, "Doesn't mean I won't always be here for you. It'll just be for the weekend too, we'll be back before you know it."

"I know," I said while pulling back and smiling up at him. "Behave yourself with Jeremy."

Those dark eyebrows of his rose as he chuckled. "You behave yourself with Porter."

I rolled my eyes as the twins walked over. I was surprised when Jeremy gave me a quick hug before waving between Porter and I. "See you guys later!"

With that they got into Jeremy's truck, pop music playing as they pulled away. "Bye," I said while watching the truck drive down the driveway before disappearing from sight.

"So uh Levi," Porter's deep voice suddenly said from besides me. After turning towards him I watched him take a few shaky breaths. "Uhm. You still feeling better?"

"Yeah," I said with a slight nod.

Ever since he called me darlin' I've been trying to stay away from him. I couldn't run the risk of getting close to him, when he doesn't know the real me. So this weekend was really going to suck, considering it was just going to be us here. Fuck my life. Being around him and only him was not going to help me get over him any easier. Having a stupid crush on him was just that, stupid. Luckily I wasn't sick anymore so I could actually leave and maybe even find someone this weekend.

"That's good," he said while scratching the back of his neck.

Before things could get any more awkward I gave him another nod before walking back inside and upstairs. Without Wyatt the house seemed so quiet already, I hadn't remembered us being apart since we were little. I also realize I was being dramatic because Wyatt and Jeremy were literally only going to be gone for the weekend. But he was basically a part of me, and I wish I was a strong enough person to stay on my own.

With a sigh I fell onto the bed, staring at the ceiling with a frown. After hearing barking from outside, I slowly sat up and moved over to the window. Porter was outside loping around on a horse, looking like he should be on the cover of a magazine.

Also since my attention span was the size of a gnat, I was already bored. And also a little hungry. I should probably not try to cook and burn the house down. With nerves in my stomach I wandered down the stairs and outside, over to where Porter was sitting on top of his horse. When he saw me he smiled, my heart doing a flip flop which only made me frown. Not only was he a fucking attractive person on the outside, but he was also fucking attractive on the inside. And it hurt my heart that I could never end up with him. Because I was so convinced once he found out everything about me, he'd want nothing to do with me.

"Hey-"

"Do you have any food here?"

His smile fell as he tipped his cowboy hat up to get a better look at me. "How about a ride first?"

He was then swinging his leg over the saddle and sliding down onto the ground. "A... what?"

"I can show you how to ride if you want, and we can get lunch after."

"I'm fine."

Once he slid onto the ground he looked down at me, a look I wasn't familiar with in his eyes. "You sure?" He then gave another smile before gently patting his horse on the shoulder.

"Is this the only way I'm getting something to eat?"

This time he laughed which only made my insides flutter harder. "Fine." I'd ride this damn horse if it meant I could eat.

"Have you ever ridden before?" After giving him a look he simply laughed. "Right, city boy. Okay first, stand facing this way and put your hands on the saddle." After taking a deep breath I did as he said as he stood behind me. "Now, I'm going to hoist you up. Lift your left leg up a little and when I start lifting you up just jump up a little and you'll get into the saddle. Okay?"

After nodding I could feel him bend down behind me, his hands landing onto my foot. Before I knew it he was lifting me up and I was swinging my other leg over until I was in the saddle. With a shaky breath I looked down and realized it was a long way to the ground, which only made me swallow hard. Porter must've sensed my fear because one of his hands landed onto my thigh, the other landing onto the small of my back.

"Look at you, sitting on a horse."

I laughed before quickly stopping once Porter got the horse to start walking. "Oh god."

"You're okay," he quietly said as his hands tightened on me.

"I already miss Wyatt," I whispered before realizing I actually said it out loud.

Porter was silent for a moment but I could feel his eyes on my face. The sudden rush of emotions hit me like a train, why was this hurting me so much? Out of the corner of my eye I could see his cowboy hat moving as he nodded. "I feel the same way about Jeremy." When he sighed I looked down at him to see him frowning. "He's been the constant thing in my life that I needed. We actually haven't been apart for our entire lives so this is so weird to me." He seemed to stare off into the distance with a sad look on his face. "And I'm happy for him don't get me wrong, I've always wanted him to find someone he can trust and love. I just really miss him but luckily they're only going to be gone for the weekend." His eyes found mine as he said, "Only the weekend."

"Right."

We fell into a comfortable silence as we continued to walk around. A little while later he finally stopped the horse and explained to me how to dismount. "Take your right leg out of the stirrup and swing it around the back side of the saddle. Your other foot will slide out and you'll slide down onto the ground."

I couldn't help but laugh before saying, "You make it sound so easy."

He smiled, those green eyes staring up at me. "I'll be right here to help you."

The only motivation I had to get off this horse was food so I quickly started to dismount. Of course I moved a little too fast and practically fell, but luckily Porter's long arms were wrapping around me to keep me upright. When I turned around in his arms and looked up at him, I completely gave in and let my hands rest onto his waist. We silently stared at each other before he suddenly took his hat off and gently placed it onto my head.

"There," he said with a smile. "Now you're a real cowboy."

We continued to silently stare at each other before I whispered, "Thank you."

"Now," he said while clearing his throat and stepping back. "Let's get you some lunch. I know a great restaurant that I really think you'd like."

"Sure."

After putting his horse away I followed him towards his truck, where we drove for about thirty minutes. My stomach growled loud as we pulled up in front of a really cool looking place. He led me inside where he held the door open for me, making my stupid cheeks erupt into a huge blush. Once the hostess saw us she smiled and straightened, her eyes lingering on Porter for a second longer.

"Welcome to The Vine, just two today?"

"Yes please, can we sit in the patio?" Porter asked as the hostess nodded.

"Of course, please follow me."

She led us through a really cute restaurant and then out onto the patio, where I stopped and gasped. The patio was basically covered by a pergola that was covered in huge vines and simple white lights. It looked like a secret garden and I honestly wasn't sure if I had ever seen anything so beautiful before.

Once I stopped walking Porter ran into me, his arms instantly wrapping around me. My hands landed onto his hands as he leaned down to whisper in my ear. "Pretty, right?"

"So pretty," I said while looking at him over my shoulder. Those green eyes were so close to mine and were only pulling me in. I could feel his solid body behind me and smell his amazing cologne, or maybe that was just how he smelled in general.

Forcing myself to snap out of it, I stepped out of his arms even though that was the last thing I wanted to do. Being in his arms always makes me lightheaded and makes me forget about everything else around me. It felt like our little moment had lasted so long, but when I look towards the table I realize the hostess was only just placing the menus on the table. Porter followed me over to the table as we sat down, her eyes still looking at Porter like she wanted to sleep with him. Get it together lady.

When she was finally done un dressing him with her eyes she said, "Your server will be right out."

After she was gone I started looking at the menu before hearing more footsteps walk up to us. Once I looked up I saw a woman walking towards us with two red roses in her hand. "Hi guys," the lady said as she placed the roses down. "I'm Rachel and I'll be taking care of you. Can I start you off with something to drink?"

Once giving her our drink orders she left, but didn't take the roses with her. "She left her flowers here," I said while trying to see if there was anyone else around.

The deep chuckle of Porter made me look up to see him smiling while holding the roses out to me. "Everyone gets a rose when they come here."

"Really?"

"Yeah, I'm not really into flowers though. I'd like you to have them."

My fingers wrapped around the roses he held out to me, knowing my face was probably the same color as them. Just then the waitress was coming back and taking our order before leaving again. I was glad the waitress left us some bread so my fingers could be busy. The way Porter was looking at me made me shove more bread into my mouth.

"So Levi," his deep voice said as soft music was playing above us. "Do you miss New York?"

Once swallowing the bread I stared down at my fingers, bad memories flooding my mind. "I miss the hustle and bustle yet... I'm getting used to the slow paced lifestyle here. That's honestly the only thing I miss, I have nothing waiting for me there."

"No significant other?"

I couldn't help but laugh while twirling a rose in my fingers. "I've never been one for relationships."

He sadly nodded before taking a long sip of his water. "I get that. Ever since I got cheated on I haven't been in a relationship. Unfortunately I've really only been about one night stands." He shook his head before running a hand through his hair. "I'm not proud of that, but I'm working on it. I've realized what I've been missing out on by not allowing myself to get close to anyone again." His eyes then found mine which only made me anxious. Why was he telling me all of this? It only made me feel that much worse since I wasn't being completely honest with him.

The kitchen must be really slow since our food came out so quickly, but I was extremely grateful for the distraction. And for the cheeseburger coming my way, the sight of onion rings making my mouth water. I looked at the rice dish Porter had before diving into mine. The entire time we were eating I kept the roses on my lap, still surprised he would've brought me here.

We kept slight conversation throughout lunch, before our waitress came back with the check. When she left I went to reach for my wallet, Porter's hand stopping me. He simply shook his head before placing a credit card onto the check.

"Let me pay half," I said as the waitress appeared out of nowhere and took it.

"No way, you're a guest."

"Well, thank you."

He gave me a smile before helping me stand up and walk back out to his truck once the waitress came back. The ride back to the farm was quiet but comfortable, my eyes trained on the beautiful scenery the entire time. Iowa was so different than downtown New York and I always thought I was going to hate a place like this. But the quiet beauty of this place was really starting to grow on me which only made me more nervous than I was before. How am I going to go back to New York where no one is waiting for me? How am I going to leave a place I was actually starting to like?

Once Porter turned down his driveway I saw a large truck by the barn, a trailer of hay attached to the back. "Who's that?"

"That's Theodore, our hay guy. We all call him Theo though. He was a friend of my dad's back in the day and has really helped us since he's been gone."

"Sounds like a true friend," I said as Porter parked the truck.

After grabbing the roses to jump out of the truck, I happened to look up and see Theo walk out of the barn. I felt the blood drain from my face almost instantly upon seeing him.

"Lev? You okay?"

When I found his confused eyes I grabbed his chin with my hand, turning his head towards where Theo was walking. "Does he not look exactly like someone we both know?"

Porter's eyes were studying the man before he quickly looked back over at me. "Wh... I... maybe this is just a coincidence."

I gave him a look before looking back over at Theo who was now taking a bale of hay off the trailer. The reason we were both speechless was the fact that Theo looked exactly like Wyatt, from the dark curly hair to the same eyes, to even the height. I'm fully aware that many people have curly hair but, it was like I was looking at my best friend. The best friend who was currently in New York. How is this even possible?

Gripping the roses tightly in my hand, I got out of the truck with Porter quickly following. Theo was then looking up and smiling, the dimples making me stop in my tracks. It was insane how much he looked like Wyatt which also made no sense to me. Ever since we were little he had never known who his father was. Whenever he tried to ask his mom about who his dad was, she would always say she wasn't sure. She said it was a long time ago and we should focus more on the future. I just wish she was still here today.

"Porter!" Porter placed a gentle hand on the small of my back, gently pushing me forward.

"Hey Theo." They shared a brief hug before Porter smiled down at me. "This is Levi, he's Kurt's nephew."

Theo smiled down at me as I studied his face. His curly hair was slightly sprinkled with gray but actually looked really nice on him. My insides were filled with butterflies just thinking about the possibility of him being my real life uncle. And if he really was Wyatt's father, did he even know? I should probably stop jumping to conclusions .

"Nice to meet you Levi."

"You as well," I said while shaking his hand. He definitely looked like a giant teddy bear, someone you could spend hours hugging. It was then that I spotted the ring on his finger and my smile fell.

Porter must've sensed my change because he quickly cleared his throat. "Levi came here from New York."

"Is that so? I hear it's beautiful up there. Are you staying here long?"

"I'm not too sure yet."

"Just know that you have the best tour guide around," he said while nodding towards Porter. Just then his phone rang in his pocket. "Excuse me; it was a pleasure meeting you. See you around Port." As he turned to walk away I heard him say, "Hey honey."

Once he was out of ear shot I turned towards Porter and whispered, "He's married?" I probably didn't need to whisper but I was still in a little bit of shock.

Porter slowly nodded before looking down at me. "And has a daughter."

"How... how old is she?"

"Twenty nine."

"That's only one year younger than Wyatt," I said with a frown.

Porter frowned as well before grabbing my elbow and nodding towards the farmhouse. "Come on; let's go watch a movie or something."

With one last look at Theo I followed him into the house, the dogs jumping up on us as greeting. They were weirdly starting to warm up to me now. Porter led me over towards the couch where he pulled me down next to him.

"This can't be a coincidence Porter."

I watched him calmly place a blanket over our laps as the dogs snuggled up next to us. "Let's not worry about it right now okay? There's nothing we can do until Wyatt gets back."

"Okay."

Even though I tried to put it out of my mind, I knew nothing was going to make me feel better until Wyatt got home. Then we'd get some answers about everything. Well, hopefully we would.

Nine

J eremy

"Hey, hey! Look what the cat drug in."

I could feel Wyatt's body next to me tremble with laughter as we walked into his former office space. Many guys had instantly jumped up to greet him the moment we walked into the office. So many people were excited to see him that it made me feel like shit that he would be away from them. I watched them all greet him with hugs and high fives before everyone turned towards me. Having so many eyes on me was making my palms instantly sweat.

"Everyone, this Jeremy," Wyatt said as he gave me a soft smile. "He's a very special person in my life."

That alone made butterflies fly into my stomach; I still didn't understand how he was always so nice. The plane to New York was pretty fun, he spent the time telling me about the different sights we'd see and things we'd do. The first stop would be his office then the sightseeing would start later. But seeing him laugh with his previous coworkers was making me frown a little. I really hope this was a decision he wouldn't regret.

They all greeted me but I could feel some not so nice stares coming my way. It made me want to sink into the ground as I slightly waved. I also felt very out of place in my cowboy boots, jeans and flannel shirt. But from the way everyone was staring at me I wish I would have just dressed not so much like a farm boy. But since all I knew was being a farm boy, I didn't know how else to dress. No one else in this room seemed like the type to wear boots or a flannel... but I was in the city. Very different from our small Iowa home.

Once all the introductions were made some of the guys went back to work as Wyatt led me towards another office. There was a lawyer looking guy inside with another guy.

"Wyatt," non-lawyer guy said as he stood up and wrapped Wyatt into a hug. "Great to see you man."

"You too Will. Jeremy, this is one of my closest work friends Will. And this is my company lawyer Mr. Wilson. Gentlemen, this is Jeremy."

We exchanged pleasantries before Wyatt looked down at me again. "I'll come find you when I'm done, okay?"

"I'll be around," I said with a smile before exiting the room.

I didn't want to interrupt him during this pretty important meeting, even though I know he'd say I could stay. He was just so nice; sometimes I wondered if he was really interested in me or just being pleasant. My mind instantly wandered to the day I taught him how to fish, how we might have kissed. And also the night outside the bar when we danced, moments like those seemed like he could really be into me. But I wasn't about to get excited over the possibility of an imaginary scenario. It was just too hard to give my heart away, again. I quickly shook my head and continued on down the hallway.

My eyes went all over the walls and stopped when I came upon a bulletin board. There were many pictures of company picnics and family days. A smile crossed my face when I saw pictures of Wyatt in a hard hat smiling next to friends, all seeming happy. It made me that much sadder that he was selling this business.

"Hey there." I jumped upon hearing a voice next to me, looking over to see a friendly looking guy. "Sorry to scare you!" He had a buzzed head and muddy brown eyes. "I'm Lenny."

"Nice to meet you, I'm Jeremy."

My eyes couldn't help but travel back to the bulletin board and all the pictures. "We've had some great memories here," Lenny said as I looked back over at him. "But I'm happy Wyatt is leaving. I love the man don't get me wrong, but he's just seemed so down lately."

"Really? How so?"

"When he first started this company he was so energetic and really into it. Lately he just hasn't seemed like himself, and really just seemed sad. It just seemed that lately his whole demeanor has changed, he really doesn't seem to enjoy being here. I mean see for yourself."

He then pointed back towards the bulletin board, first pointing to a picture from a few years ago. Wyatt's smile was bright and his face looked happy. A picture from a few years later showed a Wyatt with a smile that wasn't as bright and he didn't seem that happy. I had no idea he wasn't as happy as he was even a year ago.

"I think he'd been wanting to move for a while," Lenny's voice snapped me out of my thoughts. "But Levi never wanted to leave New York and, as I'm sure you know, they're pretty much a package deal. Of all places to end up I was surprised it was Iowa, no offense."

I couldn't help but laugh while shoving my hands into my pockets. "Non taken, I get that. Especially since he's from the city and he's somewhere pretty different now."

"Different is what he needed, really. I'm really glad he found you Jeremy. You seemed to come into his life at just the right time."

"Oh," I said as my cheeks lit up. "We're uh... not together."

Lenny simply gave me a look before shrugging. "Whatever floats your boat man; I'm still glad he found you. Even if you guys are just friends he seems so much happier than he's been."

"I just don't want people to think I'm making him move, or anything like that."

"No way man," Lenny said while shoving my shoulder with his. "Fuck what anyone else thinks honestly. Just keep doing you and make sure he's happy."

My eyes wandered back to the bulletin board. It was pretty obvious how small his smile had gotten over the years, but could I really make him that happy? He's been making me really happy since him and Levi have been with us, I get happy thinking about him. He makes me happy when I see him; I get excited knowing I'll see him again. But it's been hardly no time since we met. How could I be falling so hard for someone I barely know? If I fall this quickly now, will it just end up in more heartbreak?

The more I kept staring at the pictures of Wyatt, the more I could feel myself opening up to the idea of letting myself be vulnerable again. Just because my high school boyfriend dumped me the moment someone new moved into town doesn't mean all men are pigs. Right?

Realizing I was still just standing there I shook my head before saying, "Always."

"Really nice to meet you Jeremy, I gotta get back to work. Hope you enjoy New York."

"Thanks Lenny."

When he walked away I looked at the bulletin board one final time before continuing my journey down the hallway. I could hear multiple guys working outside before coming into a break room. A man and a woman were sitting at a table eating chips and laughing before looking up at me. I forced myself to smile and look friendly.

"Hi, I'm Jeremy."

"What's up man I'm Kyle."

The woman gave me a friendly smile before saying, "I'm Wendy, nice to meet you. I still can't believe our boss man will be living it up in Iowa, on a farm."

"We all knew Wyatt was looking to get out of this place," Kyle started while shoving Cheetos into his mouth. "And we were all hoping for the best when he took a leave of absence to take Levi to his uncle. No one knew he'd turn into a cowboy himself though."

"We're happy he did though," Wendy said as Kyle nodded. "How is he out on the farm?"

When Wendy offered me a seat I sat next to her while saying, "He's actually fit in really well to the farm life."

"Man, I'd pay to see him muck a stall," Kyle said while finishing up his bag of chips. He was then moving on to a small bag of Doritos as Wendy simply rolled her eyes at him.

"Has he worked here a long time?"

"Definitely," Wendy said. "He started in high school, worked all through-out college here as well. He kept climbing up the ladder and before we knew it he was the owner. The best boss I've ever had, that's for damn sure. We're all going to miss him around here."

Kyle nodded while running a hand through his long hair. "So true Wen. I'll take pleasure in thinking about him becoming best friends with a horse."

I laughed while saying, "I'll tell him to send you guys pictures."

"Do you want any chips?" Kyle asked as chips were falling out of his mouth.

"No thanks," I said with a laugh.

They went on to tell me a little more about the company and themselves before a voice behind me said, "There you are Jer." With a smile I turned around and watched as Wyatt walked towards me, his eyes twinkling. "You guys behaving?" He asked Wendy and Kyle.

They both laughed, Kyle saluting him. "Of course boss man."

"Not anymore," he said as I stood up next to him. "I have officially signed the paperwork and Will is now the owner."

"Are you okay?" I asked while resting my hand on his waist.

When he looked down at me he smiled, looking truly happy. "Never been better."

We stayed a little longer for Wyatt to give a proper goodbye to everyone before leaving the company for the last time. He then brought me to one of his favorite sushi places and got me to try things I've never had in my life, but it was actually delicious

"This is delicious oh my god," I groaned while swallowing a big bite of sushi.

"I'm glad you like it," he said with a smile as he leaned his head onto his hand. "Listen Jeremy, I really wanted to thank you for coming here with me. I thought I would have been okay here by myself but I honestly don't think I would have been."

"I'm glad I was here too, it was nice getting to see where you and Levi are from."

He then picked up a sushi roll and placed it into his mouth, his eyes wandering outside. "Penny for your thoughts?"

A smile broke out onto his face before he looked back over at me. "Have you ever felt like you were just in a rut? I had a good routine but that's all it was, just a routine. Get up, go to work, possibly work out and always made sure to eat dinner with Levi. Everything besides him was starting to feel stale, you know? I once had been really excited to go to work but lately I've just been burnt out. I've been starting to become a workaholic and I didn't want that." His eyes wandered out towards the center of the park again as he said, "I want something different in my life. I want to become excited again and I know if I stay here, I'm not going to find that."

I glanced down at the chopsticks in my hands before looking back up when he started talking again. "I honestly only stayed in the city for Levi, he's always been a city boy. And since I grew up here I was too, but ever since we went out to your farm I just felt like I could breathe easier." He laughed while running a hand through his hair. "That probably sounds odd; I can't even explain the feeling."

"I get that though," I said as he turned towards me. "Fresh air is really good for the soul."

A smile spread across his face as he said, "It sure is. And I want more moments that are good for my soul."

"Do you still have an apartment here?"

"I do, I've been in talk with a realtor. I just need a new start and..." he stopped talking while looking into my eyes before swallowing. "I just think it'll be good for me."

With that he took another bite of his sushi. "Okay so I have a crazy request."

His dark eyebrows rose as a smile lit up his face again. I really enjoyed seeing him smile like that. "Lay it on me."

"Can I see your apartment before you sell it?"

"Of course."

He said it so fast I laughed. "That was easy."

"You're hard to say no to Jeremy."

That made my cheeks light up as we finished our food. I was in awe watching him hail a taxi before we ended up in a really nice area. I felt bad that he spent money on a hotel, if we could've just gone to his apartment instead.

We walked inside the building and up to the tenth floor before he opened a door. He ushered me inside the quiet space, my eyes instantly looking around. It was nice; it looked pretty much out of a magazine. There was a nice looking couch, some nice blankets and a clean kitchen. I could imagine him making coffee before work and coming home and vegging out with Levi on the couch.

"Wow, a little different than the farm."

He laughed while closing the door. "Definitely. It's crazy though; I was so excited to buy this apartment and used to love coming home to it."

Leaning against the couch I turned towards him while asking, "You don't love it anymore?"

"I love the memories I had with Levi here, but I'm ready for new ones." When he started laughing I gave him a glance, wondering what was up. Before I could ask he said, "No one has ever worn cowboy boots in here before."

"Oh god I'm not getting the floor dirty am I?"

He laughed again while coming over and standing in front of me. "Not at all. Thanks for coming here with me Jeremy; I have no words to say how much I appreciated it."

"You don't need to thank me, anyone would have done it."

It seemed like he was going to say something but closed his mouth instead. "Not just anyone, but you're special."

His words were making butterflies fly around my stomach. "Not really." Before he could say anything else to make me feel like a teenager, I picked up a picture frame that was on the coffee table. "Is this your Mom?"

He looked at the frame I was holding with a soft nod, his eyes becoming sad. The picture was of a very young Wyatt and his mother sitting on a beach, both laughing. I could feel the love between them just from a single picture. "It is," he said while leaning against the couch.

"She was so pretty," I said while looking at her long dark hair and dark eyes.

"She was," he softly said. "If I'm being honest she's a big reason why I want to leave. This entire city reminds me of her and honestly it's just too much.

I can't even describe how much I still miss her, how much I'll always miss her. I just want to be somewhere new where I can make new memories."

"Do you think she would like Iowa?"

He nodded while running his thumb over the frame. "She said she visited Kurt a few times before I was born, and she seemed to enjoy it. I think just being away from the city will be a good change."

"I think so too."

He gave me another one of those smiles that made me melt before he carefully put the frame down. "I guess I should pack, huh?"

"If you have some boxes I can start helping you pack too."

"You really don't need to Jeremy; I definitely didn't bring you to New York to pack up my things."

With an eye roll I playfully shoved his shoulder while saying, "I know that Wyatt. But I want to do this, for you."

I swallowed my fear and wrapped my arms around him in a hug, his arms immediately wrapping around my waist. "Thank you, so much."

Our hug was strong and long, which was what I thought Wyatt really needed right now. As much as I don't want to be falling for Wyatt, I've definitely fallen. That thought itself was scary, but Porter's words kept coming into my mind. I needed to just chill out. With Wyatt by my side I think I could do just that.

Ten

- -

Wyatt

I smiled while watching Jeremy practically jump into his brother's arms, the twins complete again. Levi was patiently waiting for me to walk over to where he was standing by the porch before tightly hugging me. His smaller body was giving mine a very tight hug.

"How've you been Lev?"

"Alright," he mumbled against my chest. A few moments later he pulled back to look up at me. "How was New York?"

"Great actually," I said as the twins made their way over to us. "I think Jeremy bought about every single souvenir out there."

Bringing Jeremy to New York with me was the best decision I ever made, and I was so glad he came with me. With him by my side it was that much easier to simply let everything go. Because my life wasn't in New York anymore, I just had good memories there. But Levi probably wasn't going back and I wouldn't go back without him. And Jeremy also wouldn't be there, that was something I couldn't do. Since my mother also wasn't there anymore and my business was gone, I had no more emotional ties to that city. Now I was more interested in a cowboy who had given me some amazing hugs this weekend, who smelled amazing. Everything about him was amazing and I knew I couldn't have done everything in New York without him. I wish I knew just how to thank him.

Jeremy laughed, Porter chuckling as well. "There's just so many cute ones! It was hard to choose just one. Speaking of that Port can you help me bring my stuff in? I might have bought you some things."

Porter smiled while grabbing a suitcase. "Good god, did you buy all of New York?"

"Just about."

I watched them walk inside before looking down at Levi again, really studying his face. "You look really tired," I said while noticing the dark circles under his eyes. "Have a good weekend?"

"It was alright," he said with a shrug. "A little boring."

My eyebrows rose as I grabbed my suitcase. "Really? No steamy moments at all?"

He simply rolled his eyes while following me towards the farmhouse. "I don't know what you thought was going to happen. Nothing has ever happened between Porter and I-"

Right before I could open the front door I could hear a truck coming down the driveway. Levi and I both turned around to see a truck with a small trailer attached coming towards us. "Looks like a hay delivery," I said. "Think they need help?"

For some reason Levi's face fell as he quickly grabbed my arm. "Let's not bother them, come on. Tell me everything about your trip."

"Come on let's not be anti-social," I said while grabbing him and pulling him down the steps. "I left my life in New York, the least I can do is meet the people around here."

Right as the truck parked I walked down the porch steps, Levi instantly following behind me. "Hey Levi!" A deep voice said from the opposite side of the truck. "I forgot to drop off a-"

I stopped walking when I saw who emerged from around the truck. He seemed to do the same when he saw me, a strange look crossing his face. Speaking of his face I couldn't help but notice the way it seemed to look exactly... like mine. He even had black curly hair that was sprinkled with gray. Who the hell was this guy?

When a door opened behind us I turned to see the twins coming out, the smile on Jeremy's face dropping. He stopped in his tracks, Porter running into him, before his eyes slowly looked between me and the guy. He was then making his way over towards me as I turned back around, noticing the guy still looking at me.

"Theo?" Jeremy asked while stopping right next to me.

The guy, Theo, looked down at Jeremy before looking back up at me. "I..."

He then swallowed before Jeremy said, "This is Wyatt."

"Are we seriously going to ignore the elephant in the room?" Levi was asking, making Porter sigh behind me. I watched Levi walk towards us before pointing between Theo and I. "You guys look exactly alike! Like... exactly."

"Levi," Porter calmly warned.

"No, I want to know. Why the hell do you look exactly like my cousin?"

"I was wondering the same thing," I said as Theo looked back at me.

All of us stayed quiet for a long time until Porter cleared his throat. "Levi, let's give them some privacy."

"Privacy my ass."

With that Porter grabbed Levi's shoulders and pushed him away, Levi not seeming to be happy about the decision. I noticed Jeremy looking between us as he whispered, "Do you want me to leave too?"

"Please don't."

He nodded while standing next to me, giving me silent strength. "I uh, I don't know what to ask or think?" I asked Theo who still looked confused.

He slowly nodded while continuing to look me up and down, a mixed set of emotions crossing his face. "How about we go into the barn," Jeremy said.

Theo nodded while he turned around and started walking into the building. Before I could walk Jeremy placed a gentle hand onto my arm, making me look down at him. "Whatever happens I'll be here."

"What would I do without you," I said while taking a shaky breath.

With that we followed Theo into the barn, not quite sure what we were walking into. This could either be life changing news or just purely coincidental. Either way I felt like I was going to throw up. When I said I wanted a new change of pace in my life I wasn't quite expecting it to happen so quickly. Here's hoping it wasn't too quick.

Porter

"Maybe you shouldn't have been so... frank," I said after finally pushing Levi away from Theo. After a little bit I noticed them walk into the barn, not quite sure what was going to happen from that. How wild would it be that Theo and Wyatt are related? It seemed like an obvious shock to both of them.

I instantly noticed him give me the stink eye before rolling his eyes. "Okay well, my best friend deserves to know why your farm hand looks exactly like him."

With that I looked over at him while asking, "Why are you so crabby today?"

He rolled his eyes again before saying, "Excuse me, am I not allowed to be in a shit ass mood? I have to be friendly all the time?"

When he went to stomp off I gently grabbed his elbow and swung him back around towards me. "What is going on Levi?"

"Nothing," he said while shoving his elbow out of my grasp.

"Don't give me that," I said. "I've come to know you pretty well."

He gave a humorless laugh while running his fingers through his hair. "You don't know shit about me Porter. Don't even try to act like you do."

"Then let me get to know you! Or at least let me know why your mood has changed so much. You were so excited for Wyatt to come home and now that he is, you seem to be in a worse mood."

Levi frowned before sinking down onto a porch step, making me kneel in front of him. "I don't know," he whispered while staring at the ground. "My emotions have been a little all over the place recently. And just the thought of Wyatt finding his real dad, makes me emotional. He's always wanted to find him but didn't want to upset his mom by looking for him. And I don't know...it just makes me wish I had more people who love me. My parents are a joke and I don't even know why I'm here. If Wyatt learns something about Theo, where will that leave me? He'll have Jeremy and his father and I'll have..."

He adverted his eyes before quickly standing up. It seemed like he was going to try and run away, but I didn't want him to. I needed to go after him and not have him leave. Not like this. I needed him to know of the feelings that have been creeping into my mind, basically since Levi arrived.

"If you'd let me, you'll have me."

Without thinking I swallowed my fear before leaning down and capturing his lips. He didn't seem to move and basically froze, hopefully not from fear. But the moment his lips hesitantly moved I placed my hands onto his neck and deepened the kiss. His hands hesitantly gripped onto my shirt as he made soft whimpers.

When he suddenly pulled back and looked up at me, he wasted no time in making a beeline out of my arms and into the house. With a shaky breath I immediately ran after him. After not seeing him in the kitchen I ran upstairs, stopping when I got to his room. He was quickly shoving clothes into a suitcase, his face very frazzled.

"Levi," I cautiously said while stepping into the room. He ignored me while continuing to pack. "Levi," I said again while walking over to him and placing my hands onto his shaking ones. He refused to look up at me even when I gently tipped his head up towards me. "I'm sorry," I said. "I shouldn't have done that."

He shook his head while tears were starting to run down his cheeks. "It's not that Porter," he cried while running his hands over his cheeks. "I... I need to leave."

"Look Levi, I'm sorry for kissing you without consent. But I... god Levi I'm getting fucking attached to you. I know Iowa isn't your favorite but I promise it isn't bad all the time. I can take you back to New York if you're homesick-"

"I can't fucking stay here Porter!" He suddenly yelled as he ran his fingers through his shaggy hair. "I can't be around you anymore." When my face fell he said, "I can't stop these feelings I've been having for you."

"I have the same feelings for you Levi, it's okay."

"No!" He yelled while sinking down onto his bed and resting his head onto his hands. "I can't have feelings for you," he cried while I kneeled down in front of him. "I can't Porter."

With a frown I grabbed a tissue from the nearby nightstand and gently placing it on his lap. "Can I know why you feel this way?"

He remained silent as he grabbed the tissue and wiped his eyes. "Because you don't know the real me. And I..." He stopped talking as more tears slowly ran down his cheeks. "I've been living in a stupid fantasy world and I need to leave before I get in too deep."

Grabbing another tissue I gently wiped his skin off as he started hiccup-ping. "Just because I don't know the real you doesn't mean I'm just going to stop having feelings for you. I want to keep getting to know you and I promise, I'm not just going to disappear."

"That's what you say now," he said while looking down at his lap.

"That's what I'll continue to say. How about you let me know why you think I'm just going to leave before you actually leave? Because Lev, I can't have you going back to New York. Please."

He gave me a look before suddenly taking his phone and scrolling through it. After a few moments he hesitated before handing the phone over to me. After taking it from him I looked down at the screen to see a cheerleader smiling back at me. She had long blonde hair and bright green eyes and even though she was smiling, it looked sad and forced. When I looked at her eyes again I looked back up and realized they were the same cautious eyes of Levi.

My eyes wandered back down to the screen as Levi swiped to a different picture. It was the same woman as before in a senior portrait. Her hair was shorter and her smile was sadder. That was when I noticed the name under the picture, Alexis Eleanor Lutz.

When I looked back up at Levi he was crying harder. "That was me," he sadly said. "I... I was born a girl." Before I could respond he said, "My mother always wanted a girl and was thrilled when she got one. She loved to trot me around like a little show pony all dolled up. So I'm sure you could imagine the disappointment she had when I told her I wanted to be called Levi. Especially when I chopped all my hair off. She hated it and she started to hate me."

My heart broke as I wrapped one arm around him while placing my other hand onto his thigh. "I knew I was in the wrong body ever since I was little. I just knew it. I didn't want to get into cheerleading but my mother forced me. She made me do all the girly things I didn't want to do. Even when I got asked out in high school and we were going to have sex, I knew it wasn't going to feel right. I had to be one hundred percent sure though. So, I had sex for the first time with a random guy and instantly hated it. I forced him to switch to anal and honestly it felt so much better. After that I became known as the anal slut in high school."

He took a shaky breath as I wrapped my hands in his, giving them a squeeze and letting him know I was still here. "My high school was a shit show and didn't let me change my name for any yearbook. Even my teachers wouldn't call me Levi, and still called me by my birth name. Being called that name is one of the worst feelings in the world. But luckily, I graduated and got the hell away from those people. Wyatt was with me every step of the way, especially when I wanted to go on hormones. I'm not fully transitioned but plan on it in the near future. And... I've never... felt this way about anyone before. And I'm afraid because I really like you but I'm..."

"Perfect," I whispered as he just stared blankly at me before rolling his eyes.

"This is why I didn't want to say anything," he started to say while starting to stand up. "If you aren't going to be serious about it-"

"I am serious Levi," I said as he stopped moving and looked into my eyes. "You are perfect in every single way. You're the bravest person I know going through what you have in your life, and for telling me this. You're so strong."

He continued to stare at me blankly before whispering, "That's... it? How ... how are you being so calm about this? Please Porter; just tell me if you're not okay with this."

"Levi," I said as he started crying. I pulled him closer to me while saying, "I'll be honest I've never met someone with a similar story as yours. But just because I've never been in this situation doesn't mean I'm going to dismiss you. I'm a very open minded guy and honestly, this makes me like you even more. It doesn't matter that you were born a different gender, it honestly doesn't. The only thing that matters is you feeling safe and happy."

With a cry he wrapped his arms around my neck and pulled me into a hug. I wrapped my arms tightly around him as he cried into my shoulder. I had to deeply breathe while feeling tears in my eyes. "I promise Levi, I absolutely promise that this isn't something that'll make me turn away from you." Once pulling back I said, "I will always remember this day as being one of the best days of my life, because you trusted me with something so special. I'm sorry that you had to grow up with people not respecting who your true self is. But I promise that here, you will feel no judgment. Jeremy will never judge you and neither will I."

He took multiple deep and shaky breaths before slowly looking back up into my eyes. I gently wiped the tears off of his cheeks before his arms pulled me closer, our lips connecting. I then pulled back to sprinkle gentle kisses over his jaw and neck before pulling him into a hug. I then pulled back to pick him up into my arms, a smile finally forming onto his face. I then walked into my room and shut the door, locking it too. I simply planned on changing into some pajamas but once I carefully put him onto the bed he captured my lips again.

Our bodies fell back onto the comforter as his legs opened so I could get closer to him. His legs were then wrapping around my waist as he clawed at my shirt. I quickly chucked it off as his fingers were then running all over my chest before wrapping around my neck and pulling me back down. When my lips started kissing his neck again he started wiggling underneath me, making me move back a little. I watched as he took his shirt off, chucking it onto the floor.

We stared at each other for a few moments before I leaned down and started kissing all over his chest, his fingers gripping my hair. Once my lips got down by his belly button he suddenly tensed up. That made me look up to see a nervous expression on his face.

"I... I don't want you to see that part of me. I'm not there yet and I... I don't like being on my back."

"It's okay," I said while crawling back up and cradling his head with my hand. "I wasn't going to do anything and would never put you in that kind of position. This doesn't have to go any farther than this; I'm not looking for only physical things with you Levi."

His eyes got misty as he leaned into my hand. "I'm still waiting for you to realize you don't want this."

I simply gave him a look while saying, "Not going to happen. You're not getting away that easily Lev and I really hope you never go away. I want you, I want this, I want us."

His arms pulled me closer and buried into my hair once we started kissing again, his legs running up and down my jeans. "Do things to me, please."

We didn't speak again as he quickly undid my jeans and started shoving them down my legs. I had to pull back to kick them off my legs before I was left in my boxers. He was sliding his own pants down his creamy legs before throwing them onto the floor, a pair of bright yellow boxers with little bananas left. I didn't do anything with them, instead returning to his mouth to kiss him. I was insanely hard when I reached for a condom and lube, my erection straining against my boxers. When he reached for my boxers I pulled back to whisper,

"We can do that later. Let me pleasure you."

"Porter I..."

"It's okay," I said while kissing his forehead. "I know how to make love to a man."

Relief washed over his face as he nodded but watched as I lowered my bowers down. I hoped I looked okay for him, before watching as he switched over to his stomach. My lips were kissing all over his back before I whispered, "Can I take these off?"

When he nodded I slid his boxers down, kissing his neck while grabbing the lube. I coated a finger before swirling it around his entrance, his body arching up to meet me. His fingers were gripping the sheets as my finger slowly entered him, loving the heat. It made me that more excited to be inside of him.

I kissed all the way down his back before adding a second finger, his eyes closing in pleasure. After I made sure he was properly stretched and ready, I grabbed the condom and put it on myself. I then grabbed more lube before slowly starting to slide into him. "Oh fuck," I said into his shoulder as he moaned.

"Porter," he moaned as I picked the pace up a little while sliding completely into his body.

Everything was amazing and he felt so good, I wanted to make sure he felt just as good. I pulled out almost the entire way before thrusting back inside while kissing his shoulder. When I placed my hands onto the bed, his fingers intertwined with mine as I started to go faster. His body was suddenly shaking before he cried out, his body clenching around me and making me see stars. I tightened my fingers on his before feeling the familiar tingle start in my body. A super explosive orgasm rocked my body as I groaned and softly kissed his neck.

Our heavy breathing was filling the room before he turned so we could kiss, everything about this moment magical. As my now soft dick was exiting his body I kissed his shoulder again.

"Do you want to use the restroom? I promise I won't look at you, but if you want me to go first I can."

"You can go," he softly said as his head buried into the sheets, his eyes looking tired.

"I'll be right back darlin'," I said before walking into the bathroom and throwing the condom away. As I stared at myself in the mirror I couldn't stop smiling, I was so happy that Levi opened up to me. I hope he realized I was here to stay, because there was no way I could leave him.

Eleven

Levi

I stared at my reflection in the bathroom after sliding into one of Porter's shirts. I could still feel his fingers on my body, how delicately he touched me and how respectful he was. That thought alone was making me tear up again as I held his shirt up to my nose. God I hoped his smell would never leave my mind, if I could have it as a candle I would. I definitely wasn't planning on sleeping with him, but I also wasn't planning on word vomiting and spilling my guts. In a way it made me super nervous because now I felt so open and vulnerable. He said he was okay with everything and it didn't freak him out, but what if it would one day? There were lots of what ifs running around in my head before pulling my boxers up.

My eyes felt really heavy as I walked back out into the bedroom, instantly looking towards the bed. Porter was sitting on the side in pajamas, wringing his fingers together. He looked so nervous it was making me nervous as I sat down next to him. His green eyes found mine as he smiled, making butterflies swarm into my stomach. Even though we just did the most intimate thing, every time he looked at me felt intimate. It felt like he could see right into my soul. Which was pretty terrifying.

"Having regrets?" I asked.

"What? No, why would you think that?"

I shrugged while saying, "Just figured."

"Levi, I don't have any regrets." His fingers were gently resting onto my face while giving me a look. "Don't fill your head with that okay? I'm not going to regret anything we do together, ever. I'm mainly just worried that you're thinking we rushed into being physical together. I should've taken things slower."

"If you haven't noticed I don't really like going slow, my patience is thin." A smile spread onto his face as his fingers ran over my cheeks. "I've wanted to touch you since I got here and now that I have, I'm not going to be able to stop."

"You can touch me any time you'd like darlin'," he said as his fingers slowly ran over my cheek. "And I wasn't joking Levi, I'm in this. I want you and more specifically I want you in Iowa." His fingers wound up in my hair as he brought our foreheads together.

Tears were suddenly stinging in my eyes as I pulled back to look into his eyes. "Are you sure this... me... doesn't bother you? I know you're saying you're okay with this but, I want to be certain."

"You have nothing to worry about Levi, please believe me." With that he pressed a kiss onto my forehead. "I'm not just going to instantly change my mind just because we slept together. I'm not an asshole."

"I know," I said while taking a shaky breath. "You just have one."

A loud laugh was filling the room as he pulled me in for a hug, my arms tightly wrapping around him. "You're so clever," he whispered against my hair.

Just being in his arms was making me feel so... seen. He was so open and accepting of what I told him, which most people wouldn't have been okay with. He already knew the most intimate thing about me, but I really wanted him to know truly everything. This way if he does end up thinking it's too much, at least I didn't keep any secrets. I was just hoping he wouldn't think I was too much, not after I fell for him. I'm not sure I could come back from that.

"I got a mastectomy," I nervously said. After taking one of his hands I gently placed it onto my breastbone, his fingers slowly running over my shirt. "Since my mom still thought what I was feeling was 'just a phase', she didn't agree with anything I wanted. So she kicked me off her insurance but since I didn't have a job I didn't have any. Thank god Wyatt helped me; I don't know what I would've done without him. He made really good money at his company and paid for it without a second thought."

That thought made me cry, even though I tried to hold it in. Porter's fingers wrapped around mine as he placed a gentle kiss onto my head. "I knew from a very young age I was different, something wasn't right. I grew up with Wyatt basically as a brother because we're so close, and I always wanted to be just like him. My mom hated I turned into a tomboy and would play baseball and football with Wyatt, but I loved it. It was something that made me feel like... me. I didn't want to play dress up in fancy dresses like my mom wanted me to. And she couldn't understand that, still doesn't. She won't accept me for the real me, I'll always be a daughter to her."

"I vividly remember staring at myself in the mirror and truly hating what I saw. I kept asking Wyatt why I didn't look like him, the way he looked was how I felt inside. He didn't think I was weird for asking, or when I cried the first time I had to buy a bra or when I got my period. Here I was stuck in a body that wasn't mine and I didn't know what to do. My boobs kept getting bigger so I would tape them to go as flat as possible, Wyatt knew how much they affected me. He surprised me with an envelope of cash on my birthday and when he told me what it was for, I cried. I felt bad though and didn't want him to pay for the other huge surgery I want."

"He's a good man," Porter said while running his free hand slowly up and down my back. "I'm so grateful you had him growing up and that he saw you. Thank you for telling me Levi. And I'll be here for you every step of the way, I promise."

With tears still in my eyes I pulled back to kiss him, crawling onto his lap. After a few kisses I slowly took my shirt off again, letting it fall onto the bed behind him. This time his hands slowly ran over my chest before he leaned forward to kiss my skin.

"Is it odd I really like these scars?"

"Of course not," he said as he kissed said scars. "They got you closer to feeling completely like yourself. And might I add, they look amazing on you."

"You don't have to butter me up; I am planning on sleeping with you again."

He laughed again as his arms wrapped tightly around my waist. "I'm not buttering you up Levi, just being honest."

"Thank you," I whispered as he lowered us onto the bed.

He stared at my face as my eyes suddenly felt heavy. "Why don't you rest? I'll be here the entire time."

"Promise?"

"I promise," he said before kissing my cheek.

With that my head rested against his chest as his fingers ran up and down my spine. Usually I didn't feel comfortable being shirtless around anyone, but Porter was different. He made me feel the same way Wyatt did growing up- seen. My whole life I wanted someone to look at me the way Porter did. I could not let myself fuck this up, because I knew no one else would make me feel as safe as this man. With Porter's arms tightly around me I was able to drift off to sleep, the best sleep I've ever had.

Wyatt

"Since we have the same face I'm assuming you and my mother got together at some point?"

Theo ran a hand over his face as he nodded. "Yes, I loved Rachel very much."

"Loved her?"

"I know it's probably silly," Theo said with tears in his eyes as he sank down onto a hay bale. "We barely knew each other but from the first moment I saw her I wanted her. She came out here for the summer to visit Kurt and we ran into each other. One thing led to another and ever since then we were inseparable. I was trying to convince her to stay in Iowa once the summer ended but... she didn't want to. She loved city life and didn't want to give that up. She really broke my heart when she left, but I had no idea she was leaving with you. I never heard from her again," he ran his hands over his face as his shoulders started shaking. "I can't believe she was pregnant and didn't tell me, I would have moved to New York for both of you. There's no way I would have let a child of mine grow up without a father."

Seeing him start to get emotional was making me feel emotional, for the father I never knew. "Words can't express how deeply and truly sorry I am," he said after looking back up into my eyes. "When she went back to New

York I never heard from her again. From your expression I'm assuming she never told you anything about me?"

"Nothing," I said. "She always made it seem like she didn't know who my father was, let alone remember his name."

That seemed to hurt him as he frowned and shook his head. With a humorless laugh he ran a hand through his curly hair. "I, I can't believe this. She knew I would have done anything for her. Maybe that freaked her out because we had only known each other for a little time. Do you think she'd be open in having a conversation about this?"

I felt my heart drop as Jeremy gently held onto my arm and gave it a small squeeze. He gave me silent strength as I met Theo's eyes again. "Kurt... didn't tell you?"

"Tell me what? And I'm not really one for sharing too much information with other people. He knows I'm married and have a daughter but I try not to get too personal." When I remained silent he looked between Jeremy and I, frowning. "What is it?"

"My mom passed away from a drunk driver when I was ten."

Theo's face fell immediately as his eyes watered with tears. "What? Rache l's... gone? God I'm so sorry Wyatt."

Jeremy's arms tightened around mine as I said, "Thank you."

"You've been alone since you were ten?" When I nodded his hands ran through his hair, tears now actively running down his cheeks. He then started pacing while putting his hands on his hips. "Why wouldn't she tell me? Why did she hide a son from me?" I then watched as he kneeled down in front of the hay bale Jeremy and I were sitting on. "I understand if you don't really want anything to do with me. I can't make up time for not being with you your entire life, but I'll be here. I am so sorry about your mom."

"Thank you," I said. "I'm not really sure what I feel like, just feel overwhelmed."

"Understood," he said with a slight nod. "If you need anything, I'll be here."

"I think I just need to be alone for a while."

It seemed like he was going to say something else but simply nodded and stood up. "Jeremy has my number if you need me."

When I nodded he gave me one final look before walking away. My head dropped into my hands as the tears finally came. My entire body shook as Jeremy wrapped his arms around me and pulled me into him. I wasn't even sure how long I just sat there and cried. Cried for the father I didn't know I had, yet he was here. My entire childhood. And I never knew.

"I can't believe she didn't tell me," I cried into Jeremy's shirt. "Why would she hide something like this from me?"

My body continued to shake as I cried harder. I had no idea how long we were sitting there but I needed this. When my tears finally stopped and my body stopped shaking, Jeremy helped me stand up. He kept one arm securely around my waist as his other hand landed onto my stomach. We walked like that inside before he carefully helped me onto the couch. He grabbed a nearby blanket to drape over my lap as he went back into the kitchen.

Once he reemerged he was holding some water and snacks, placing them onto the coffee table. "I haven't had a lot of experience with friends, so I'm not quite sure on how to comfort people. But Porter always brings me snacks when I'm sad. I know this isn't going to make you feel better, but

I hope it's a start." He then wrung his fingers together while saying, "I'm sorry Wyatt." His eyes were misty as he gently placed a hand onto my cheek.

I placed one hand on top of his, resting my forehead on top of his. "Thank you. Just thank you for being here."

He then gave me another hug before turning the TV on and flipped to a random movie. My heart was still beating wildly but sitting next to Jeremy was making me feel better. It was going to suck but I needed to go talk to Kurt. That was a conversation I wasn't looking forward to.

Twelve

L^{evi}

Something tickled my face, making my eyes slowly and sleepily open. However the instant they did my heart all but flew out of my chest. Porter was leaning above me leaving kisses over my face. Once my eyes became less fuzzy I realized he was wearing what looked like barn clothes.

"Morning darlin'," he said with a smile.

"Morning?" I croaked while running a hand over my eyes. I didn't think it was even nighttime when I fell asleep earlier.

"You slept a pretty long time, but I think you needed it. I wanted to let you know I'm going to be out in the barn if you need me."

A stupid smile lit up my face as I wrapped my arms around his neck and pulled him down to my level. When his lips captured mine my fingers wound up in his hair. I loved feeling his strong body above mine and the feel of his lips on mine. It was worrying how much I liked him, literally everything about him.

When he pulled back he ran a hand over my flushed face. "I didn't want you to wake up alone."

"You're so sweet," I whispered while running my fingers over his scruffy face.

He smiled before kissing my wrist. "Wyatt told me last night he was going to go see Kurt today. I wasn't sure if you wanted to go with him, he said he was leaving sometime around noon."

"I'll probably go," I said with a yawn. "Even though your bed is so comfy."

"I liked waking up with you in my bed, liked it a whole fucking lot."

"Just wait until I'm in your clothes. Then you'll really never want me to leave."

His face softened as he leaned down to kiss me again. "You can always wear any of my clothes, anytime you want. And no, you're not leaving, even if I have to tie you to this bed."

My eyebrows rose as I said, "Didn't take you for the kinky tying up kind."

He laughed while saying, "Not really my thing but if you're into that we can always explore it."

With that he kissed me again, even softer than before. "Can I explore more of your body tonight?"

"I mean I'm not going to say no to that."

I smiled as he kissed my cheek again. "Are you okay with me... telling Jeremy about us?"

"Of course. I wanted to make sure you were okay with that until I said something to him."

"I was uhm... also going to tell him about me."

His fingers slowly ran over my cheek before his thumb ran over my bottom lip. "I promise you he won't be nasty to you at all. You know how he is; he's very open and loving to everyone. Do you feel comfortable talking to him alone?"

"I think if we could do it tonight, like all of us. Would that be okay? I just, feel really comfortable around you guys here. And I don't want him to be left out."

"Don't think you need to tell him if you're not ready. But that's absolutely okay with me. Maybe we can order a pizza too."

With a nod I wrapped my arms around him in a hug. "I'm ready."

"I'm so proud of you." He then kissed my neck before smiling down at me again. "I might not see you before you go to the hospital with Wyatt. If I don't I'll see you later okay? You'll come home, to me?"

My heart pinged and my eyes watered as I nodded. "I will."

He smiled before kissing me again. "Then I'll see you later darlin', tell Kurt hi for me."

With that he slowly got off the bed before leaving, a smile still on my face. It took a little while longer to actually roll out of bed and get dressed, but I took my time. Mainly because I loved how his bed smelled like him, everything did. I still couldn't believe he said that about coming home... I still didn't understand him. He can't possibly be real. And if he is really real, how the hell did I get so lucky to end up here? I felt like I was going to wake up from this wonderfully blissful dream at any moment. Might as well enjoy it while I still could.

Once I was finally dressed I walked downstairs to see Wyatt sitting at the table drinking coffee. He had dark circles under his eyes as he looked up at me and nodded. "Hey," I said while sliding down in front of him.

"Hey. Didn't see you last night."

"I slept with Porter."

He immediately started coughing, his eyes wide. "What the fuck? Are you serious?"

"Yes."

"The last I knew nothing had even happened between you two. How did that happen?"

With a shrug I pulled my legs up on the chair before wrapping my arms around them. "He just makes me feel so... seen. I've never felt this way about anyone in my entire life."

"So I'm assuming you told him?" When I nodded he asked, "And I'm assuming he took it well?"

"Surprisingly well." I explained how Porter had kissed me and everything he had said after I told him. "How can someone just be so cool with everything? I mean it wasn't like I told him I had an embarrassing tattoo or something, this was deep."

"People do that when they care about someone, truly and utterly care."

I chewed on my bottom lip while saying, "I showed him my chest scars. I didn't show him... me you know? But he saw half of me."

"I'm so damn proud of you Levi."

One of his large hands then gripped onto mine. "Thank you. Sorry for everything that happened with Theo yesterday. How are you doing?"

He sighed before drinking more of his coffee. "I don't even know. There's just so many thoughts swirling around in my head. I was so overwhelmed last night; I thought I was going to throw up. Jeremy stayed on the couch with me all night but I couldn't sleep. I wanted to go ask Kurt some things."

"Are you going to be super pissed if he knew about Theo?"

"Fuck if I know. This is all new to me."

"Well yeah, not every day you find out you've had a dad when you thought you didn't. Is Jeremy coming too?"

"He told me he's going to help Porter with the chores."

With a nod I said, "Speaking of him, I'm going to tell him tonight. Porter was talking about getting a pizza and you know, just making a night of it."

"Do you want me to be there too?"

"Well duh."

"It sounds nice; it'll take my mind off of things."

We ate some food before finally making our way out of the house. I could see Porter in the barn, the dogs dancing around him. He was currently moving a bale of hay as Jeremy laughed next to him. The sight made me smile; it was so nice seeing them every day. What would I do if I couldn't see them? Just thinking about that made my chest tighten up and my palms start to sweat. God damn, what was wrong with me? I hadn't even known the twins for that long and yet I was already so invested in both of them. I hope it didn't end up biting me in the ass.

"Levi?" I snapped out of my thoughts as Wyatt stood in front of me.

"Sorry, what?"

"I asked if you were ready to go."

"Yeah, let's go."

We got into Jeremy's truck and made the trip to the hospital. I was getting nervous for Wyatt as we parked and walked inside. After walking towards Kurt's room I poked my head inside to see him staring out the window. When he turned and saw us he smiled, his face completely lighting up. It'd been so long since someone had been excited to see me; it was always odd when someone smiled like that. It made me think back to Porter this morning; he seemed excited to talk to me. Ugh, I needed to stop overthinking everything.

"Hey guys," he said while sitting up a little more in bed.

"Hi Kurt," I said while giving him a hug.

He must've noticed Wyatt's weary expression as I sunk into a chair. "Everything alright?" Kurt asked as Wyatt sat next to me.

"Did you know Theo was my dad?" Damn, he didn't waste any time in asking that. When Kurt remained silent Wyatt frowned. "You knew? You knew and didn't tell me?"

"I didn't know for sure. I didn't even know your mother was pregnant for a while. After her visit out here she left pretty abruptly and I thought she was just homesick. Plus your mom wasn't really the farm type, always a city girl. Theo wasn't really around the farm a lot when he was younger and your mom didn't bring you here. I only pieced it together when I saw you for the first time. You looked exactly like him, still do."

I looked over at Wyatt who was still frowning. "You knew I wanted to know who my father was, I always did. And my mom never told me for some reason, she always made it seem like she didn't know who he was. Why didn't you tell me after she was gone?"

"The first time I saw you, I asked her if Theo was the father. She eventually said he was, but didn't want him in your life. She wanted to raise you by herself and didn't want me to tell you. Then after the accident you hardly came out here. I'm sorry Wyatt, I should have said something."

Wyatt stood up while running his fingers through his hair with a sigh. "If you would have told me I wouldn't have come face to face with a guy who looks exactly like me. I got blindsided Kurt. How could you not tell me? First my mom lied to me then my uncle. What's the point of having family if they're just going to lie to you?"

"Hey," I said. "I've never lied to you."

He turned towards me with a softer expression. "I know."

"And if my sister wanted me to keep something a secret, no offense, but I'm going to go with my sister. I'm sure she had her reasons, even if they weren't the best. But Kurt's literally the only family we have left."

"I never wanted this to divide us," Kurt said. "But I understand if you need time away. I am really sorry Wyatt."

"Knock knock!" I watched as Debbie then walked in with a big smile. "Oh hi Levi, Wyatt."

"Excuse me," Wyatt abruptly said before disappearing from the room.

Kurt sighed before running his hands over his face, which was looking pretty tired. "Hi Debbie," I said as she started to check over Kurt.

"Hi dear," she said with a smile. "How are you feeling?"

Once I first arrived I had asked her some questions about the doctors here, if any had ever worked on a transgender patient. There apparently was one, only one, but that's better than nothing. She told me more doctors would probably come in to help with the surgery. I'd been biting at the bit to get my bottom surgery; I wasn't going to rest until I did. I just couldn't afford it. So I would be stuck with this body part at least for a while longer.

"I'm good," I said with a nod. "How are you feeling Kurt?"

"I have good days, and I have bad days."

"Is today a good or bad day?"

He shrugged but smiled like nothing was wrong. "I'm alright."

"Are you sure?"

He finally smiled a real smile before nodding. "Don't worry Levi, I'm fine."

Looking over at Debbie I asked, "Is he really fine?"

She gave a small chuckle before saying, "He's getting stronger and today is definitely better than it's been for him."

When he started yawning I got up and gave him a hug. "I'm going to go find Wyatt. I think he just needs some time, but I'm sure he'll come around."

Kurt gave a sad smile. "I hope, but I'll understand if he doesn't."

After that I gave Debbie a goodbye wave before walking out of the room, no fucking clue where Wyatt went. Just as I was about to call him I happened to walk outside to see him sitting on a bench. Walking out and sitting next to him I stared at his tired face before looking out at the flat land around us.

"I just don't get why she would have wanted to raise me alone," he said shakily. With a frown I wrapped an arm around his back as he continued. "Why would you hide the fact that you know who your child's father is? She knew I was so damn curious about him, and the way she always acted she didn't even know his name. Yet now I find out that I've actually had a dad and he's been here... the entire time. He went on to have a family and didn't even know about me. I mean it'd be one thing if he knew about me and just didn't care, but he didn't even know. And the other only family member I love besides you knew, and didn't tell me." He then ran his hands through his hair.

"I feel like I'm not going to have the right thing to say," I said with a frown. "Mainly because I don't know what to say. We'll never know why she didn't tell you but at least you grew up with one parent who truly loved you. You know she would have done anything for you; maybe she didn't want to share you. I don't know if you're aware but you're pretty fucking awesome Wyatt. And you now get to learn all about your dad, which is pretty cool. I mean he wants to be in your life, he'll be here for you whenever you're ready. And maybe you'll never be ready but I think you should give him a chance at some point. I think it'll be good for not only you but him too."

He remained silent for a second before wrapping his arms around me in a big hug. "Thank you. All of this has really exhausted me, ready to go?"

"Yeah," I whispered.

The ride back to the farm was quiet, Wyatt staring out the passenger window the whole time. Once we parked he walked inside the house, grumbling about wanting to lay down. Before I could follow him I noticed Porter in front of the barn fixing a fence. My heart instantly started beating faster as I made my way over to him. Once he saw me coming he smiled, pushing his cowboy hat up while walking over towards me.

"Hey," he said while wrapping his arms around me.

"Hi."

"Everything go okay with Kurt?"

"Eh," I said with a shrug. "I think things are going to be a little... messy for a bit."

He frowned while his thumbs ran over my shirt. "I'm sorry. Is there anything I can do?"

Shaking my head I buried my face into his shirt, loving the smell of him so goddamn much. My fingers dug into his back as I whispered, "Just don't leave."

"I'm not going anywhere darlin', I promise." We stayed in a comforting hug for who knows how long until he asked, "Want to learn how to feed some horses?"

"Feed them?"

"Come on city boy," he said while pulling me into the barn. "I'll make a country boy out of you yet."

I laughed when he winked at me but inside I was dying. "We'll see country boy. If I do a decent job can I still do stuff to your body tonight?"

This time he laughed before leaning down to kiss my lips. "I will never deny you that."

He was then pulling me towards the stalls, his hand on mine the entire time. He really didn't know just how attached to this country boy I was. Hopefully I wouldn't do anything to mess that up.

Thirteen

Jeremy

"Pizza will be here soon," Porter called into my room after I got out of the shower. I wasn't sure why he wanted to meet up tonight, but I was glad food was involved.

The mood around the house had been a little glum ever since Wyatt found out about Theo. I didn't blame him; it was a lot of information to receive and some pretty earth shattering information at that. Honestly I wasn't sure how I didn't instantly think of Theo the first time I saw Wyatt. I was just really taken aback by how attractive he was. Everything about him- his curly hair, his dark eyes, and of course those tattoos. One day I'd love to trace every single one on his arm. I wanted to be braver around him but also didn't want to push him. This was a pretty sensitive time for him, and I didn't think he had the time for me at the moment.

After throwing on some pajamas I wandered downstairs to see Levi and Porter sitting on the couch. I was happy they had been getting along so well, Levi seemed to like farm life more than when he first arrived. Just then the doorbell rang, making me walk over and grab the pizza. As I went to turn around I all but ran right into Wyatt, who instantly steadied me. His strong arms were steading me as a pretty smile lit up his face.

My body was suddenly having such a strong reaction to him I had to close my eyes. Just seeing him in soft pajamas with damp hair was making the lower half of me act like it's never seen an attractive man before. I suddenly had a very big urge to touch him. My god, what was my problem? I've been around attractive men before but he... he was different.

"Are you okay Jeremy?"

Oh god, him saying my name was not helping the situation. Seriously, what was wrong with me? I suddenly felt so ashamed I wanted to hide in a corner and cry. I forced my eyes to open to see Wyatt staring at me with a worried expression. After blinking a few times I realized my eyes were wet, god I was a mess.

"Fine, sorry for almost knocking you over."

He laughed, a husky laugh that made goosebumps run all over my skin. "No worries, it's good."

"I should uhm; put the pizza in the kitchen."

With a nod he stepped back but followed me into the kitchen. I was very aware of his presence behind me as I put the pizza box onto the table. When I turned around to grab plates I watched him get drinks, his tattoos seeming to shimmer. It seemed like my body was acting on its own as I slowly walked over to him.

My index finger was then reaching out and landing onto his skin, his body instantly freezing. I could tell he was looking at me, probably because I was acting like a damn freak. I just couldn't leave this kitchen without touching him. There were so many cool swirls on his skin that only made me want to explore them more. My body suddenly stopped and realized how creepy I probably looked, dropping my hand to turn away.

Before I could leave he reached out and brought my fingers back to his skin. His hand was then holding onto mine as he traced my fingers over his skin before I shyly looked up at him. "S-sorry," I stuttered. "Your tattoos are just really cool."

"Don't ever apologize," he said. "You can touch them whenever and wherever you like."

My heart was beating so loud in my chest I was sure he could hear it, but I didn't care. However before I could say anything else Porter was suddenly yelling, "Hey Jer, can you bring some pizza in here?"

That snapped me out of the trance I had been in, my cheeks probably lit up like a Christmas tree. "Yeah," I croaked out while turning away. I quickly grabbed some slices and put them on plates before walking out into the living room.

Once the pizza and drinks were distributed, I plopped down into a chair as Wyatt took a seat next to Levi on the couch. Right as I took my first bite Levi was suddenly looking over at me, an unrecognizable expression on his face. "Before we start there's something I wanted to talk to you about Jeremy," Levi said.

"Go for it," I said with a smile after swallowing my pizza.

He suddenly looked nervous before Wyatt grabbed his hand. "Uhm well first off I think you should know Porter and I..." He opened and closed his mouth multiple times before my brother spoke up.

"Are an item."

I smiled while looking in between them. "Really? That's great you guys!"

That made Porter smile as he wrapped an arm around Levi. "There's more," Levi said. "I'm transgender."

"Really?"

"Yes, I've known since I was little I was in the wrong body. There's nothing quite like knowing you were born in the wrong body, and not being able to do anything about it. Once I was old enough I started taking testosterone and I got my top surgery. I just wanted you to know, especially because I'm looking to get bottom surgery soon."

I quickly put my plate on the coffee table before walking over to the couch. Porter moved over so I could wedge myself in between Levi and Wyatt, before wrapping my arms around him. He hesitated a second before wrapping his arms around me as well.

"Thank you for feeling comfortable enough to tell me. I can't even imagine how scary that must've been. If there's anything you ever need I'll always be here for you."

After a few moments Levi pulled back, his eyes watery as he softly laughed. "All my life I've had people tell me this was 'just a phase', and I'd feel different later. Then I came here and I meet you two, just thank you." He returned to our hug before softly starting to cry. Porter wrapped his arms around Levi from behind in a hug, Wyatt's left arm reach over to comfort him. Since I was in between them his right arm was wrapping around my waist, his chest pressed against my back. He felt so solid behind me I had to take a couple deep breaths before I could re-focus.

"Thank you for coming here," I said while his arms tightened around me.

The four of us stayed in a group hug before we continued to eat while watching random shows. Levi then said he was going to go shower, giving Porter a look I didn't want to know what it meant. When he was gone I suddenly realized Wyatt's right arm was still wrapped around me, and I had actually scooted back against him more. I told myself to not freak out and also to not get freaky thoughts, it was just a hug.

"When do you think Levi will get his bottom surgery?"

"He's been really stressed about the money," Wyatt said with a sigh. "I told him I could help him but he refuses for me to pay for it."

I then slowly turned my body so I could look up at him. "That was really sweet of you."

"I'd do anything for him," he said while looking right in my eyes.

His fingers were then slowly running over my shirt before Porter said, "I wish we could just win the lottery or something. There has to be a way for this to work out."

"Oh, wait!"

I almost fell off the couch and onto the dogs as I spun around and looked at the wall behind us. "Jer what the hell is your-" Porter stopped when he looked to where I was looking, a thoughtful expression on his face.

"Uhm what's happening?" Wyatt asked. "Is this some twin thing going on?"

"This painting," I said while walking over towards the wall. "Remember this Port? Dad always said if we ever needed money this painting was the key."

"That's right," Porter said. "Apparently this painting has been in the family, for that reason. It's the just in case painting. Isn't it by Patsy Snow?"

"Really?" Wyatt asked while getting up and coming over to it. "Her paint-ings are super rare and hard to find."

Porter nodded while gently touching the frame. "Especially because she's up there with Van Gogh, god I can't believe I forgot about this. And it was in plain sight all along."

"We just have to find a person who won't take advantage of it," I said. "We need to find a legit dealer. Oh my god do you think we could get enough money for the surgery this way?"

"Since she's as famous as Van Gogh I'd say yes," Wyatt said. "And if it doesn't I'll drain my savings for Levi. He's gone through too much shit, he deserves this. But are you guys sure?"

Porter instantly nodded. "Of course. I know how important this is to him, and he deserves to be happy. I'll gladly drain my savings as well. I'm going to go tell him." A smile lit up his face as he ran up the steps two at a time.

Wyatt was suddenly giving me a hug, making me laugh. "God you're the best."

"Don't get too excited, hopefully we can get enough for it."

"Even you coming up with an idea like this, just thank you."

His face finally seemed less stressed as he pulled me back over towards the couch. We ate more pizza and watched more movies while googling art dealers. I was so excited I was practically shaking; I could only imagine how Levi would feel. I couldn't wait to see his face if we're actually able to pull this off. I knew my dad was the one to plant this idea into my head and for that I'd always be grateful. He was always looking out for us before, and always will be. I hope one day Wyatt could get that kind of feeling from Theo.

Porter

My body was shaking in excitement as I walked into my room, but stopped short. Levi was on the bed, currently wearing one of my shirts and boxers that had stars over them. He was in such a deep sleep I didn't want to wake him; he'd been having pretty dark circles under his eyes. Instead of waking him I shut the door and turned the light off before getting behind him on the bed, my arms wrapping around him.

I'd never felt this attached to someone before, I never had people stay over in my bed. But Levi could stay here as long as he wanted, hopefully a long time. I didn't want to freak him out with how deep my feelings were, I just couldn't help how my heart felt. The even sound of his breathing was helping me to drift off to sleep, still so damn excited about our plan.

*

The feeling of something tickling my neck made my eyes slowly open, instantly seeing Levi straddling me. It was still dark outside and the house was quiet, probably the middle of the night. His lips continued to slowly kiss my neck as I smiled. "What a way to wake up."

He laughed while pulling back. "Sorry for falling asleep. I know I told you I wanted to basically jump on you, I've just been so tired lately."

"Don't apologize Lev," I said with a yawn. "I'm glad you've been getting really good sleep."

"I didn't want you to think I'm just a lazy piece of shit all the time. In New York I had been so stressed all the time I barely slept. Then I came here and... I just feel really safe. My body has been basically recovering from New York and I just feel a lot better."

I ran a hand over his face before leaning up to kiss him. "I can't even tell you how happy that makes me feel. I love that you're feeling safe enough to actually get sleep. You could sleep the whole day and I'd never think you were a lazy piece of shit. I didn't want to disturb you earlier; I knew you were probably tired. But I actually had some news."

His eyebrows rose up as my fingers ran over his hips. "What is it?"

"Jeremy remembered the painting in the living room; it's been in our family for a long time. It's an original by Patsy Snow."

"Are you shitting me? She's such a legend."

"Definitely not shitting you. It's actually been a 'just in case' painting in our family. Just in case we needed money that was there so we could use it. Jeremy instantly thought of helping you and getting your bottom surgery. I'm sure he and Wyatt were looking up art dealers when I left the room."

Levi remained silent for such a long time I thought I made a terrible mistake, until he started crying. "You would do that, for me?"

"Of course Levi, I wasn't joking when I told you I'm here to stay. And if the painting doesn't cover the whole costs Wyatt, Jeremy and I will come together to get it. We'll make this work darlin', we will. We all just want you to be completely comfortable in your skin."

He cried again while wrapping his arms around my neck. I simply held him while he cried before he suddenly said, "I'm sucking your dick for that then you're fucking me."

"Shit Levi," I said with a shaky breath. "But again, don't think you need to do this just because we might have found a solution."

"I'm not, I just really fucking like you."

He was then pushing me onto my back, making me laugh again. I watched as he yanked on my shirt, making me take it off and throw it onto the floor as he slid my boxers down. It was barely a second before his mouth was suddenly on me, his amazing mouth. He took me to places no one ever had taken me; he was basically sucking on me like I was the last thing on Earth. My fingers ran through his hair as I deeply groaned. Before I could go over the edge he pulled off me to straddle my lap, slowly rocking his hips with mine. As my lips captured his again I quickly grabbed the needed supplies before starting to move him onto his stomach.

"Wait," he said.

"Are you okay?"

He remained silent for a minute before saying, "I want to do it like this, I want to see your face."

"Are you sure?"

"Yeah," he said with a nod. "I'm... I'm not quite ready to be on my back yet but if I'm like this, it'll be okay. Plus your shirt is large on me so it covers that part of me. I'm just sorry I can't show you-"

I instantly put a finger over his lips to stop him. "Do not apologize for literally anything, especially something like this. This is your decision, no one else's. Only you can determine when you're comfortable enough to show that part of yourself. And honestly I don't want to do anything with it because I know it isn't you. But just know it's not going to make me not want to do anything physical with you. You just need to be open and let me know how exactly you want to do anything physical. Let me know if you don't feel comfortable or if anything feels odd okay? I'm never going to rush you Levi, that part of you isn't my prize. Knowing you're happy is my prize."

Tears were running down his cheeks as he started kissing me again. After a few minutes he suddenly got off the bed and lowered his boxers. I couldn't see anything except those creamy and gorgeous legs, which I wanted to be wrapped around me. He then climbed back onto the bed and straddled my waist as I grabbed the bottle of lube. I picked the shirt up in the back so I could have access to him, making sure to keep the shirt lowered. Even though I wanted to be inside of him right now, I'd never do that without preparing him first.

I gently kissed him as one finger entered him, his fingers tugging at my hair. By the time I had a second finger inside he was moaning and writhing on my lap, which was making me even more excited. Once he was finally prepped I rolled a condom on myself and watched as he grabbed me and lined me up with his hole. He then met my eyes as he slowly lowered his body down, both of us moaning.

Having him be in this position I could see his eyes, how they looked when he was completely overtaken by passion. I kept our pace slow and the thrusts gentle, feeling something pass through us. It seemed like we were even closer than before, if that was even possible. I wanted to explore it more though.

It didn't take much longer before both of us reached our peak, his fingers in my hair and my fingers on his shirt. His body shook from his intense orgasm as I gently kissed him again. His arms were then tightly wrapping around my neck and pulling me even closer to him. His body was then shaking but from crying this time. I made sure to pull out of him as gently as I could before holding him tight against me.

"Don't leave me," he cried into my neck.

"Absolutely never," I said while kissing his hair.

I held him while he cried and he actually ended up crying himself to sleep. I gently moved him onto the bed next to me, making sure his shirt was down the whole time. I then quickly cleaned myself up before gently waking him. I didn't want him to feel gross all night but wasn't going to clean him up while he was asleep. No way was I going to violate any boundary.

He went into the bathroom and cleaned up, before returning to bed with boxers back on. I had slipped my pajamas back on and simply held him as he clung onto me very tightly. My fingers slowly ran up and down his back before my body was starting to drift off to sleep.

Before I was in dreamland I heard a soft voice whisper, "I love you."

Fourteen

W yatt

My fingers shook while holding the phone in my hand, so many emotions running through my mind. With a deep breath I punched in the number and held the phone up to my ear, nervously biting my bottom lip. "Hello?"

Theo's voice made my body freeze and tense up; I still wasn't used to this. I was talking to my father... my actual father. Someone who didn't even know I existed until a little bit ago, someone who actually wanted to be in my life. Would it be too weird to get to know a parent after all these years? What would happen if he found out more about me and actually didn't like how I turned out?

"Hello?"

But then again, I'd never know until I found out. "Theo, it's Wyatt."

"Wyatt," he happily said. "It's so good to hear from you. How are you?"

"I was actually wondering if you would be able to meet up sometime?"

"Of course," he immediately said. For some reason that made me feel a lot better, knowing that someone wanted to see me and hopefully get to know me. "I hope this isn't too forward but, how about today? You can come out to my house."

I took a shaky breath before running my free hand through my hair. "I... I'd really like that."

He then gave me his address before saying, "I'm so happy you reached out Wyatt, I'm so excited to see you."

I had to swallow the large lump in my throat; it was still wild that I was actually talking to my dad. It'd be one thing if he knew about me but still didn't give a shit, but he didn't know I was even born. This had all been really hard on me but I can't even imagine what he's been going through. "I'm excited as well."

With that we hung up, my hands nervously starting to shake. As I wandered upstairs to change I tried to calm down my breathing. The last thing I wanted to do was look like an idiot in front of him. After walking into my room I changed, then changed again, and then tried to tame my hair. It didn't work because my hair was just too curly and too wild, making me sigh in frustration and angrily whip my fingers out of my hair. My clumsy fingers knocked over the picture frame on the dresser, the one of my mom and I.

As I bent down to pick it up I noticed the back had popped off a little. That also made me sigh in frustration because I needed to calm the fuck down, before I broke everything valuable to me. But as I lifted the picture frame up, something other than the back was poking my finger. My eyebrows scrunched together as I flipped it over to see a piece of paper. It felt like my world stopped when I realized it was a note, written by my mom.

My lovely Wyatt,

I am so incredibly proud of the young man you've turned into, there are no words to describe just how much I love you. Seeing you turn into such a fine young man makes me realize you're such a better person than I am, and you're not even a teenager yet. You've been asking about your father for quite some time now. I need to confess that I do know who he is, he just doesn't know about you. Please don't hate me for this, even though you have every right to. His name is Theo and he works out in Iowa, he's one of the sweetest people I've ever met. We got together over the summer and when I left Iowa, I also left with you. I didn't tell him and I never told you. Seeing your face and how it's identical to his, I know I did the wrong thing. All my life I've never thought I was worthy of anyone like him, we were young when we got together. I knew he would follow me to New York because I didn't want to live in the country, I'll always be a city girl. But he was so happy out in the country, I knew he would hate moving. And he obviously deserved someone a whole lot better than me, someone who didn't run away with his child. I never should have left without telling him and I never should have kept him from you. I'm writing this out because I'm so terrified to actually say these words out loud to you, I just know you're going to hate me. If it makes you feel any better I hate myself. I'm going to give you this tomorrow and hopefully fly out to Iowa soon. I want you two to meet; I know he's going to love you. You're so easy to love Wyatt. And you have your entire life ahead of you to do great things. Maybe even move to Iowa to be with your dad, and if you'll have me, I'll move out there too. There are no words to say how sorry I am. But I will always love you more than anything on this planet, I hope you remember that.

My entire body felt numb after I read it, and after reading it twenty more times. My mouth tasted like metal as I made my way down the stairs. Jeremy had told me he was going to be with Kurt all day and drove Porter's truck, giving me his keys if I needed them. Thank god for him. I was still feeling weirdly numb as I got into the truck and drove away, the note firmly in my pocket. I was expecting to cry or be angry but honestly, I just felt tired. I was emotionally wrecked.

My hands started to shake as I pulled up into a driveway, a nice little ranch style house staring back at me. Once I was getting out of the truck I watched as the front door opened and Theo stepped out. He smiled wild, giving me a wave as he walked down the front steps.

"Wyatt!" He happily said while walking over and standing in front of me. "Was the drive over okay?"

The note was suddenly feeling like a million pounds in my pocket as I nodded. "I uhm... I..."

"Wyatt," he softly said. "Don't feel like you need to feel a certain way around me. You're allowed to feel creeped out or mad, you might not even want me in your life."

"No Theo, it isn't that. I uh found this."

With that I handed him the note, his eyebrows rising as he gently took it from me. I watched his face the entire time he read it, watching a range of emotions splash all over his face. When he was finished he placed a hand onto the truck and sighed before looking at me. A ton of emotions suddenly hit me at once, like a brick to the face, that I broke down. I don't know why but I walked forward and wrapped my arms around him. His arms immediately circled around me as he held me. I could imagine him hugging me when I was little, if I fell off my bike or won a competition or just because. I'd wanted this for so long and now that he was actually hugging me, it still didn't seem real.

He then pulled back slightly to put a strong hand onto my cheek, his eyes looking directly into mine. "If I had known about you when you were born, I would have moved across the country to be there for you. I can promise you that Wyatt. I am happy that you were able to have your mom when you were little; I know she loved you so much. She always loved things and people with her whole heart. I want you to know that you might not have had a father growing up, but you'll have one for the rest of your life."

That made me close my eyes as fresh tears rolled down my cheeks as he pulled me back into a hug. He simply held me as I hiccupped into his shirt, giving me the silent and physical strength I needed. When I was finally able to pull back I wiped my eyes while saying, "I haven't cried this much in my entire life."

"Crying is good for the soul; we all have those moments where we feel down. But the important thing is that we have people around for those moments." He then gave me smile before asking, "Would you like to come inside?"

"Yeah, I would."

He led me inside where I was immediately hit with such a warmth it made my chest tighten. As we walked into the kitchen I saw two women standing by the sink. They immediately looked over and smiled as I stopped in my tracks. Theo gave me a look to make sure I was okay, seeming to feel better when I nodded at him.

"Wyatt, this is my wife Marie and my daughter Kathryn."

They both walked over but stood a respectable distance away as they smiled at me. "Hi Wyatt, I'm Marie." Her brown hair was cut into a short style that accentuated her face, her blue eyes twinkling.

"And I'm Kathryn but you can call me Katie," my half sister said. She also looked just like Theo, the man had some crazy genes. Her black hair was long and silky around her shoulders, not as curly as mine but still pretty wavy. Her brown eyes were filled with what seemed like happiness, making me realize she was looking way up at me. She was pretty short, a little shorter than Levi. Marie was only a little taller than her, I guess I was the one who inherited the height.

"It's nice to meet you," I said with a small smile.

"If you need anything or if you're hungry at all just let me know," Marie said. "I can whip up whatever you'd like."

"Thank you, I'm okay for now though."

"Of course."

Theo then motioned for me to follow him out to the back deck, where rocking chairs were set up. We sat down as my eyes took in the beautiful scenery around us; I never thought I'd enjoy country life. I also never thought I'd ever leave New York or that I'd actually have a half sister or a dad or... a step mom. Life really is crazy, for the most part it didn't make any sense.

"You doing okay?"

Theo's voice snapped me out of my thoughts as I looked over at him. "Yeah, well, as okay as I can be after finding out life altering information. But I just feel that... maybe everything is going to be okay."

With that he smiled while saying, "I feel the same way Wyatt."

*

Theo and I talked for who knows how long on the porch, just enjoying each other's company. I told him I'm gay, he said as long as I'm happy it doesn't matter who I love. I told him all about my business and then how I sold it, how I'm falling for Jeremy. I told him about my awful family, except Kurt, and how close I am with Levi. I also told him Levi is going to freak out when he realizes he has an actual uncle. Of course I didn't tell him about Levi being trans, mainly because it isn't my business to tell. But Theo listened to everything and also told me about life growing up out here and when he met my mom. When she went away and told him not to follow her it broke his heart, but Marie put it back together. The fact that he was so happy in his life with a wife and daughter, made me happy.

By the time I finally stopped talking the sun was actually starting to set, actually making me a little sad. Theo must've seen my face because he said, "We'll meet up again in a day or two, I don't want you to get sick of me already."

We were laughing as we walked over to my truck, Marie and Katie giving us a wave from the steps. I wasn't quite ready to talk to them and honestly I wanted to be greedy and have my dad all to myself. But when we made plans to have a barbeque in two days, I knew I was going to get to know them more. They seemed like really nice people.

"Be safe driving back," Theo said as he gave me another hug. His hugs were fierce and powerful, everything a father's hug should be.

"Thank you, I'll see you soon."

With that I got in and drove off, my mother's note safely tucked back into my pocket. After I got back to the ranch I walked inside to see Jeremy putting containers into a basket, smiling when he saw me. I wish he knew what that smile did to me.

"Hi! I packed a picnic, thought we could eat it on the pier." His cheeks then lit up and he adverted eye contact.

"You have no idea how much I want to do that."

He smiled before picking up the basket, giving me another smile before we walked outside. Once we were sitting on the pier he handed me a sandwich before I gave him the note I found. "I found this inside the picture frame that my mom's and my picture was."

His eyebrows shot up into his hair before his mouth dropped open. "Oh my gosh, how are you doing?"

"Surprisingly okay," I said while looking down at the water. "After that I went and saw Theo." I then detailed everything he said to me, a soft smile forming onto Jeremy's face.

"I'm so glad that you have him in your life Wyatt. And Marie and Katie are really nice; I know you're going to love them."

"We're having a barbeque in two days and I'd love for you to come."

He smiled as the wind softly blew his hair. "Really?"

After nodding I slowly inched closer to him while talking. "Really. I... I wish I could describe the way you make me feel Jeremy. It's like I've been missing a piece of me my entire life, and you're that missing piece."

His face immediately was covered in a beautiful blush as he looked down. My finger slowly brought his face up so I could look back into those eyes. "No one's ever said anything like that to me before."

"If you're okay with it, I'll gladly say things like that to you every day. I've been trying to hold myself back from you but honestly Jeremy, I can't anymore. Fuck, I'm so attracted to you it isn't even funny." His cheeks lit up with another blush. I then gently moved my hand so it was cupping his face, his face immediately snuggling into my hand. "And if it's okay with you, I'd really like to explore these feelings more with you." When he looked down and frowned I thought I had blown it. My hands started to sweat, damn it, I shouldn't have pushed it. "I'm sorry, that was probably too forward."

"No it's just... I don't know what to do. I've had those feelings too but I've never been experienced in that department. I've only dated one guy who broke my heart and since then I've pretty much shut my heart off to people. I don't know why you would actually be attracted to someone like me when you're over there looking like a literal god."

That made me bring his face back up so I could look into his eyes. "Have you even looked at yourself in the mirror Jeremy? Can you not see your beauty? And it's okay if you don't have this kind of experience. Honestly I've never been so attracted to someone before, you make me feel like a giddy teenager when you walk into the room." I gave a soft laugh as he smiled. "If you want to, we can learn these things and feelings together. Is that something you would be interested in?"

He looked into my eyes for a while longer before nodding. "I don't know where to even start though Wyatt."

"Well, how about we start with a kiss?"

His eyes got wide for a second before he looked at my lips before quickly looking away. God he was so fucking adorable. When he met my eyes again he nodded, giving me permission to move closer to him. My eyes watched him as I slowly leaned down and moved towards him even slower, in case he wanted to back out. But he didn't move, he simply watched me get closer until his eyes closed. Once my lips landed onto his it felt like my body was home. There were such strong sparks that I've never experienced, I knew I wanted to only kiss Jeremy.

His arms hesitantly wrapped around my neck as I kept exploring his mouth, absolutely loving his taste. I loved how his fingers were in my hair; I kept imaging us lying in bed and him running those fingers through my curls. My arms wrapped around him and pulled him even closer, my heart beating so loud I was sure he could hear it.

After a few more moments I slowly pulled back, resting my forehead on his. It took a few more minutes for his eyes to open and when they did, I could see all of the raw emotion inside of him. In this moment I felt like I was looking into his soul, his beautiful soul. My fingers then started tickling his sides, his laughter filling the air around us. I'd take things as slow as Jeremy wanted if that meant I could be with him. There was no one else I ever wanted to be with; he calmed my body and mind down from one of the most emotionally stressful day of my life. And having him here next to me now, his laughter in the air, made me realize that everything was going to be okay.

Levi

My eyes slowly opened as my limbs stretched onto the bed, my entire body feeling so... happy. I felt even happier when I felt the arms and body of Porter around me. I definitely wasn't expecting to have gotten so emotional when we were making love but Porter made me feel so safe. There was something so deeply personal having been able to actually see his eyes and face him. No one has ever looked at me the way he does, or makes me feel the way I've felt since I've been here. And plus, cowboys are fucking sexy as hell.

I smiled when lips were suddenly slowly kissing my head and neck before I turned around. My smile dropped when I looked at his face, something seemed off. Even though he was smiling, something looked different. Porter leaned down to kiss me before he said, "Good morning."

Oh god, he didn't call me darlin'. Did I disgust him last night? Maybe me crying and telling him to not leave was a major turn off. Maybe he finally realized he doesn't want someone like me. Unless he's just upset that the physical side of our relationship can't be like everyone else's? Or maybe that's it, maybe he doesn't want a relationship after all.

"Levi? Where did you go?" One of his large hands landed onto my cheek as he looked into my eyes. "Come back to me darlin'."

"Sorry," I whispered. "Your expression scared me."

His thumb slowly ran over my cheek before saying, "There is something I want to talk about."

"I knew it," I said while sitting up and backing away. "I told you you'd have second thoughts about dating someone like me."

"Whoa," he said while scooting closer to me. "Don't fill your head with those thoughts Levi. Just because I want to talk doesn't mean I've changed my mind okay? You need to trust me. Do you really think I'm that big of a dick?"

"No," I immediately said while frowning. "I'm sorry Porter." My arms wrapped around my legs as his fingers ran over my arm. "My default emotion is to always get defensive."

He nodded before saying, "And I can see that because the people around you growing up weren't the best. But I want you to feel comfortable here and with me, I'd never do something like sleep with you then just leave." I heavily sighed before nodding. I did have to get better at that. "I wanted to talk about last night. Right as you were falling asleep you said something and I wasn't sure if you remembered."

"From your expression I'm not sure if I want to know."

He softly smiled before suddenly moving so his arms were on either side of me. He was basically blocking me off from escaping, ugh, I must've said something super embarrassing if he was worried about me running away. "You said you loved me." My eyes got large and I tried to get away but his arms kept me in place.

"I'm sorry," I said as my heart started beating so loud. My stomach was in so much knots that I thought I was going to throw up.

"And why are you apologizing?"

"I was really emotional last night and it must've slipped out. I've never said that to anyone before, especially after uhm sex."

"So you don't love me?" His big shoulders shrugged as he said, "Well that's too bad, because I love you."

His words hit me in the face as instant tears pricked my eyes. "You do?"

"I do, I love you Levi." My arms immediately wrapped around his neck as I pulled him closer to me. His arms tightly held onto me as he said, "I love all of you and I'll always be here for you."

When I pulled back I was full on crying now. "I love you Porter, I've never loved anyone before."

He smiled before leaning down to kiss me. It was a soft and gentle kiss that made my toes curl and my entire body erupt into goosebumps. He then looked me right in the eyes while saying, "Can you please promise me that you'll stay here, and not go back to New York?"

This time I rolled my eyes while lightly shoving his shoulder. "Why would I leave when we just professed our love to each other?"

He shrugged, a faint of a smile on his lips. "I haven't allowed myself to get close to someone like this again. The last time I was in love that person really destroyed me and..." His eyes dropped to the bed as he laughed with no emotion. "I'm still insecure I guess."

"Hey," I said while putting both hands onto his cheeks and lifting his eyes back up to me. "The only other person I've said I love you to was Wyatt if that means anything to you. When I love someone, I love them with my entire heart. There's never been anyone in my life like you, no one I've gotten close to like this. I'm sick of meaningless fucks in my life and for once I've met someone who I feel really sees me for the person I am." His fingers landed on top of mine as I started crying again, him slowly wiping

the tears away. "You're the person I would give anything to not lose and...
that scares me Porter. I've never felt a love like this before and I promise
I would never leave." As more tears ran down my face I took multiple
breaths. "And besides, there's only room for one slightly unstable person
in this relationship and I can hold that position so much better than your
country ass."

With that he threw his head back and laughed before resting his forehead
on mine. "Levi, what am I going to do with you." His fingers slowly ran
along my skin as he looked into my eyes. He then slowly kissed my nose,
jaw, eyelids and cheeks before smiling.

"You can do whatever you want to me."

He laughed when I straddled him, his back falling back into the headboard.
"Then I know exactly what to do."

"Oh yeah? What's that?"

"Love you for as long as you'll stand me."

"Well you better get ready for the long haul there country boy, I'm not
going anywhere."

He smiled before wrapping his arms around me in a hug. "Neither am I."

For some reason that made my heart flutter and made me hold onto him
tighter. I definitely knew I wanted him to see all of me, holding nothing
back. This was the man I wanted for my entire life, he meant so fucking
much to me. And even though that was still scary, love was actually over-
powering the fear. I had never felt so... content before.

With that I slowly scooted back onto the bed, his dark eyes following mine.
I then took my shirt off, my fingers digging into the fabric before I dropped
it. My heart was beating wildly as I gripped the top of my pants, his eyes

getting big. Before I changed my mind I slipped them off, wanting to cover myself. The sudden shame made me burst into tears before his long arms wrapped around me and pulled me closer. He pulled back slightly, gripping my hands that somehow ended up in my lap, acting like a blanket.

"You don't need to feel ashamed Levi, never feel like this around me okay? I know this isn't your body but it will be, you're so close darlin'." His thumbs slowly ran over my skin as he smiled. "If I thought I loved you before, I love you so much more now. Thank you for feeling open and safe enough to show me."

"I want you to see me, especially because you're stuck with me for... well a long time. It's not how I look inside my head but I-"

When I started to cry again he pulled me into his chest to whisper, "I know Levi. I know." He gave me the softest kiss before asking, "Can I look at you?"

I nodded, the nausea still going strong in my stomach but Porter was making me feel a lot better. With that I slowly slid my shaking hands off of my lap before falling onto my back, completely exposed. And while normally I'd be shitting bricks by now his quiet strength was making my hands slowly stop shaking.

I watched him the entire time his eyes roamed over me, before his eyes were replaced with his hands. They slowly slid over my skin before he eventually replaced his hands with his lips. There wasn't anything sexual about this; this was the kind of intimacy that I wasn't used to. He kissed every square inch of my skin, even the part that I hated. The way he was looking at me and touching me was making me hate that part a little less.

By the time he had touched and kissed every part of me, I was emotionally wrecked. He carefully put my clothes back on and held me more. I had no idea how someone like him could come into my life and completely change it for the better. For the love of god I better not do anything to fuck this up.

Fifteen

J eremy

The sunrise caught my eye as I finished up with the morning chores, the pinks and yellows looking so elegant in the sky. I came out earlier than I usually do in the morning, but I barely slept last night. Wyatt and I stayed out on the pier for a long time last night, just enjoying each other's company. I enjoyed being around him so much I didn't want to ever go back inside. But once we finally did he kissed me in the doorway and made my heart skip a beat. I hadn't seen Porter at all last night and didn't want to barge into his room and bother him and Levi. I couldn't wait to tell him all about what happened.

Since it was still early and I was still too keyed up to fall back asleep, I decided to make breakfast. I lost myself in cooking basically everything we had until I heard footsteps coming down the steps. Right as I turned around Levi walked into the kitchen, giving me a small smile.

"Hi Jeremy."

"Hey," I said while turning back to the blueberry pancakes I was working on. When I didn't hear Levi move or walk around I turned around to see him standing by the table, biting his bottom lip. "Is everything okay?"

He nodded before saying, "I just wanted to talk to you about something."

"Go for it."

After a few moments he said, "I want you to know that I love Porter." A faint smile touched his lips; I don't think I've seen him look this happy since he's been here. "I just want you to know that I'm not just using him for a quick fuck or whatever. He's really important to me and I wouldn't do anything to screw this up. I don't want you to think that I'm going to be like this douchebag of an ex, I'd never cheat on him. And I'm not going back to New York, there's nothing for me there. But everything for me is here." He gave a soft laugh before gently wiping his eyes. "Sorry for word vomiting like that. I swear I'm not usually this bad, but I've gotten so soft since I've been here I swear."

"No it's okay," I said while moving the pancakes to a plate. "Thank you for telling me all of that. You know, Porter is usually the protective one out of the two of us. Well, the more protective one. But I've gotten really protective of him since he got his heart broken. I saw the way he acted with his ex and let me tell you, it's completely different than the way he acts with you. I've never seen him this happy and content and that's all because of you. I'm really happy you two found each other, your faces just light up around each other."

He smiled brightly before saying, "Thank you Jeremy. He's the first person to... actually love me just for being myself. All I have to say is your dad did a really great job raising you two."

That made me feel super emotional as I turned the stove top off. "Thank you," I whispered before laughing while wiping my eyes. "That's the nicest thing you could tell me. My dad would've loved you Levi, you two would've gotten along so well. He taught Porter and I how to be respectable men from a young age. And it sucks that he was taken too early."

Levi frowned before saying, "It's always the good ones that leave too early. I'm still sorry Jeremy. I've never had any feelings towards my Mom, especially not love, so I've never been able to connect to people who had or have good relationships with their parents. But the way you and Porter talk about your Dad is truly something else; I can tell how great of a man he was. It just makes me realize that not everyone in this world is shit, there's good ones."

My mind instantly wandered to Wyatt, his dimpled face smiling at me after a kiss. "There are," I said with a nod. "Speaking of good ones, I uhm... well I'm really into your cousin."

His eyes lit up as he smiled. "Ugh finally! He's been crushing on you since we first got here."

My cheeks got hot as I asked, "Wait, really?"

"Oh come on Jeremy, I never thought he was being subtle. But are you guys together?"

"Well, I mean, uhm we're taking things slow. But since you said all those things to me about Porter, I wanted you to know that I'm not planning on simply using Wyatt either. He's important to me as well; no one has ever made me feel this way before. He deserves so much."

Levi nodded before saying, "But so do you Jeremy." With that he walked forward and hugged me, his cheek only coming to my chest. "We've all been through a lot of shit but I really think we're all where we're supposed to be."

"I agree with that." We hugged for a little bit longer before pulling back. "Want some food?"

"Abso-fucking-lutely. I can bring some to Porter too. Sorry he didn't help you with chores this morning."

"It's fine, sometimes I like to just be alone."

"That's how I always felt, until I found love. It's a crazy thing." He started smiling again before grabbing two plates worth of food. "Thanks Jeremy, you're the best."

I laughed as he left the room, hearing him all but run up the stairs. After grabbing some pancakes I walked back outside and sat on the pier while looking at the water. I ate the pancakes in a peaceful silence for a while longer before watching the sky while skimming my toes on the water. When I heard footsteps behind me I turned, thinking it was Porter but saw that it was Wyatt.

My heart instantly started beating faster while looking at his wild curls, his sleepy eyes and dimpled cheeks. God, he was so attractive. It was still crazy to think that someone who looked like an actual god could be into me.

"Morning handsome," he said while sitting down next to me. My cheeks instantly lit up as he leaned down and kissed my cheek.

"Hi," I whispered while burying my face under his neck. His arms wrapped around me as my fingers wound up into his shirt. "Your shirt is so soft," I said, not really sure why I said that.

His head rested on top of mine as his fingers slowly ran over my arm. "You can wear it whenever you'd like."

I slowly pulled back to look into his dark eyes, his fingers softly touching my skin. "Wear your clothes?" I asked with a smile. "Do you have any hoodies? Because I really like hoodies."

"Hoodies huh? I have a particular one I think you'd like."

His fingers were still running over my skin so softly, it was like he was worried he would break me. "For such a large man you're so gentle," I whispered while intertwining my fingers with his.

He smiled while saying, "It's because of you Jeremy. You never seem real to me, I always feel like I'm in a dream when around you."

My face buried back under his chin, sure my cheeks looked like a Christmas tree. "If you keep saying things like that my cheeks will never stop blushing."

His fingers were then slowly lifting my face back up so I could look into his eyes. "I'll never stop complimenting you Jeremy. And I never want to stop seeing your blush, your absolutely beautiful blush." When my cheeks lit up his fingers ran over them again. "The sunrise this morning reminded me of your cheeks. Absolutely stunning." He then kissed my forehead before saying, "I caught up with Levi before I came down this morning. I also talked to Porter who told me him and Levi are having an art dealer come here to appraise the painting. Would you like to go into the city today? I'd love to take you on a proper date."

"A proper date? What exactly happens on one?"

"Has no one ever taken you on one?"

"The only 'dates' I went on were group dates or horror movies."

"Mm," Wyatt said while running his fingers through my hair. "You deserve to have proper dates the rest of your life. Would you be okay with going on a little adventure?"

I smiled while nodding, already getting excited. "I'd love it."

He then stood up and helped me up as well before we walked back into the house. We separated to get dressed, with me freaking out with what the hell to wear. I wasn't exactly sure what we were going to do today so I was having a lot of trouble trying to figure out how to dress. Right as I changed into some casual clothes a knock came from the door.

"Yeah?"

Porter's head then stuck into the room before he walked in and shut the door behind him. "Hey," he said while sitting down onto the bed. "You heading out?"

"Yeah, Wyatt and I are going to be gone for bit. He said an art dealer's coming here?"

He nodded while running a hand through his hair. "Yeah she's going to be here later, hopefully it goes okay." He then patted the spot next to him on the bed, making me come over and sit next to him. "I just want to make sure Wyatt's been nice to you."

"Of course he's been nice Porter. Do you really think I'd spend time with someone who wasn't nice? But, where is this coming from?"

"I just want to make sure; I'll kick him in the balls if he's mean to you. And I saw you guys out on the pier and you looked cozy."

I couldn't help but roll my eyes before saying, "I'll kick Levi if he's mean to you."

He simply gave me a look before saying, "You wouldn't hurt a fly."

"Doesn't mean I wouldn't stand up for you if someone else treated you like shit. And yeah, we're definitely closer than we were. We've even... kissed."

"Finally! I knew you two would end up getting together. And you don't have to worry, Levi isn't like that. He makes me feel so happy Jer, it's a feeling I can't even describe.

"I know what you're talking about," I said. "That's how I feel around Wyatt."

He smiled before putting a hand onto my shoulder. "I'm so happy for you Jeremy, you deserve it. But I wasn't kidding- if he tries any funny business I'll be coming for him."

"God Port you sound like a mafia boss or something. Trust me, Wyatt isn't like that." Before he could respond I wrapped my arms around him in a tight hug. "I'm really glad you're so happy."

"So am I," he said while returning the hug with just as much power. "Have a fun day okay?"

"You too," I said while pulling back.

Before I could get up he put his hand on my shoulder again. "Sorry I haven't been around as much. How about tonight we get some burgers and just talk? I'm interested in how you two finally got together."

I couldn't help but laugh as he smiled at me. "That sounds good. And I know you've been busy with Levi, I just didn't want to bother you."

He frowned while saying, "You know if there's anything you need you can come find me, right? Always. You and Levi are the most important people to me; I'll always make time for both of you."

"I know Port. Do you want me to get the burgers?"

"No," he said while laughing. "I'll make them later tonight; don't feel like you have to rush with Wyatt. And if you guys have a really fun night and it goes into the morning, just tell me you don't want any. I'll take that as you're having a fun night."

My cheeks lit up as I shoved his body, his deep laugh filling the room. "Ugh Porter."

"Oh come on Jeremy, it'll happen eventually. And I don't want to be a cock block."

"I'm definitely not sleeping with Wyatt tonight or doing anything... sexual. And even if I did I wouldn't tell you."

"I won't pry. Just make sure he doesn't pressure you into anything okay?"

I was about to make a snide comment until I saw just how serious he was. "Don't worry Porter; he's not the kind to rush someone. But if he does I'll tell you and you can go all Kung Fu on him okay?"

He laughed as we both stood up from the bed and started to walk into the hallway. "You bet I will."

"Have fun with the art dealer."

"On the phone she sounded close to one hundred so I hope she doesn't keel over before she gets here."

"You're terrible."

"I speak the truth."

With that I rolled my eyes, playfully shoving him before walking down the stairs. Wyatt was standing in the kitchen with Levi, both looking up as we walked in. Wyatt walked over towards me with a smile as Porter stood next to Levi.

"Ready to go?" He asked while moving a piece of hair off my forehead.

"Yeah," I whispered with a smile. Looking over at Levi and Porter and seeing them giving me a thumbs up sign, I grabbed onto Wyatt's elbow and started to pull him out the door. "Bye guys!"

"I hope you don't mind if I drive?" He asked as we walked towards my truck. "I want you to be relaxed and comfortable today."

"Fine with me." As we slid into the truck I asked, "Where exactly are we going?"

After he started the truck up he said, "Someplace with fish."

"An aquarium!?" I excitedly asked while he started to drive off the farm, softly laughing. "Or wait do you mean a seafood restaurant?"

"I'll keep it a surprise for the next forty minutes."

The drive was peaceful, the GPS on his phone speaking every now and then. By the time we got to our destination I was so excited to see an aquarium. When we got to the front entrance and I tried to pay he quickly lowered my hand. He simply thanked the woman who gave us our tickets and wrapped his arm around my waist.

"I don't want you paying for everything," I grumbled into his shirt. "I can pay for things too."

"I know you can. How about this, the next date you can get? I just really want to woo you today, because you deserve that."

My stomach filled with butterflies at the thought of going on even more dates with him. A smile crept onto my face as I said, "You deserve to be wooed too. So fine, next time it's all on me okay?"

"Pinky promise," he said while holding his pinky out.

I laughed while grabbing onto his pinky and shaking it. "Penguins!" I all but yelled while pulling him over towards an exhibit.

I wasn't even sure how long we stayed in the aquarium, it was all so fun I lost track of time. There was something about standing right next to Wyatt and having his arm around me. Or the way I'd catch him looking at me, or the kiss he would leave on my cheek or lips. I felt like such a giddy teenager the entire time I was pretty sad by the time we were done. But before we could leave Wyatt pulled me into the gift shop. We ended up buying stuffed animals for each other to remember the day. He bought me a penguin and I bought him an otter, again feeling like a giddy teen.

Once we left the aquarium we found some food trucks, a chocolate shop and a really cool little antique shop. From the antique shop I found a really cool pocket watch for him, buying it and storing it securely in my pocket, but he wouldn't tell me what he found. I saw him with a bag but he wouldn't let me look inside.

"It's a surprise," he said with a smile.

The final stop was actually to a drive in movie, which was also getting me excited. After we got popcorn, drinks and candy we got back into the truck as little kids laughed and ran by us.

"What movie are they playing?"

"When I looked it up earlier it was Casablanca. Is that okay?"

"I don't think I've ever seen it. Is it good?"

"It's a classic," he said with a smile. "I have a feeling you'll like it."

Since there was still some time before the movie started I reached into my pocket and held out my hand. "I found this at the antique shop." I watched him take the pocket watch and slowly run his thumb over it.

"Oh wow," he said. "This is gorgeous. Thank you Jeremy, I love it."

With that he kissed the side of my head as I asked, "Can I see what you bought?"

He laughed before reaching behind him and digging around for a second. I kept my penguin firmly against my chest while watching him gently place a stack of envelopes in my lap. Before I could ask anything I realized there was writing on the front of the envelopes, all in different hand writings. One said My dearest Lionel. I quickly and gently opened it, realizing it was a letter.

Lionel,

I'm lying here dreaming about the next time I'll be able to see your face. You are absolutely the best thing to have ever happened to me, thank you for making me so happy. I can't wait to start our lives together, to be able to see you every single day and call you mine. I don't know how I got so lucky. I know we're going to see each other soon but it isn't soon enough. And you're making me act and talk like a love struck teenager. But I just can't imagine not having you in my life, so I guess I am a love struck teenager. I can't help it though; you're a good man Lionel. You're the best person I've ever met and love you with my entire heart. I can't wait to see you again.

Your other half,

Gracie

I looked at the next envelope to see it was another love letter, and another one behind it. In fact the entire stack was love letters and love post cards. Some were pretty faded but the love pouring off of all of them was enough to make me want to cry. When I looked up at Wyatt he was looking nervous before saying, "I thought of you when I read these. The man working there told me these were found in estate sales all over the country. Some of them date back pretty far, and I know it might be an odd gift but-"

Before he could finish I leaned forward and kissed him, wrapping my arms around his neck. When I pulled back I said, "I love this so much. Thank you Wyatt."

Casablanca was soon starting, making me scoot closer to him. We shared popcorn and our drinks, our stuffed animals close by. With his arms around me it felt like we'd done this a million times. I couldn't wait to keep going on adventures with him like this. I also couldn't wait to tell Porter. I felt like Gracie, a love struck teenager. The right person will do that.

Sixteen

- -

L^{evi}

My stomach was in so many knots it felt like I was going to throw up. Again. I've never been this nervous before. It'd been a couple of months since Porter and I declared our love together and we couldn't be stronger. With Debbie's help I was able to find a great doctor and a team of nurses who couldn't wait to help me finally transition all the way.

I then glanced over at Wyatt, who was quietly talking to Jeremy in the corner. I had gone to the barbeque at Theo's place with him, Jeremy and Porter. Meeting my real life uncle was awesome, especially because he was such a cool person. I was really happy that Wyatt had him in his life now. The fact that he found a letter from his mom hidden in a picture frame was also wild. Even if he was upset when he first found it, his heart was too big to ever stay mad at her.

Wyatt and Jeremy were also a really cute couple, there isn't anyone else I could picture them with. And while Jeremy clammed up whenever I try and ask how the physical side is going, Wyatt luckily told me. Not everything, but at least something. I want to know because I'm a nosy bitch, leave me alone. Apparently they haven't done anything besides kiss yet, god damn, I couldn't move that slow. But I know Wyatt didn't want to rush Jeremy at all which was really sweet.

My eyes wandered back over to Porter sitting right next to me, his fingers giving constant support on my arm. When he saw me staring at him he smiled, leaning down to kiss me. I'd been so worked up last night the only way he could calm me down was to take a long ass shower with me. He then took a long time exploring my body with his lips, making me feel so seen and loved. I also loved looking into his eyes while we did anything sexual. Since I had shown myself to him we've slept together multiple times and every single time it felt like the first. I loved him so much it hurt.

"You doing okay?" He softly asked.

"I just want it to be over."

"It will be soon darlin'. And the next time you wake up you'll be exactly how you've always seen yourself in your mind. I'm so proud of you."

Tears were stinging my eyes as I pulled him into a hug. Not too long after I pulled back after hearing, "Knock, knock."

"Kurt!" Porter and I said as he gingerly wheeled himself into the room.

Wyatt and Jeremy came over as well, all of us giving him and Debbie a hug. He'd been getting slowly better as well, and was actually scheduled to leave the hospital in a week. When I told him when my surgery was I didn't think he'd actually come down here. But seeing his smiling face was making me feel better.

He hugged me last and gave me a super long and hard one. "You holding up okay?"

"I'm alright," I said while pulling back and leaning against the pillows behind me. "Scared shitless."

He grabbed my hand and gave it a big squeeze. "We'll all be here for you when you get done. I'm so excited for you Levi; this is going to be such a turning point for you."

"Thank you Kurt."

We all chatted with each other for a little while longer before a nurse knocked on the door. "Okay Levi," she happily said with a smile. "We're going to start getting you prepped for surgery."

"I'll take that as my cue to skedaddle," Kurt said before giving me a hug. He then kissed the side of my head while saying, "I'll see you later Lev."

Wyatt then came over and gave me a giant hug. "I love you Levi. Don't give the surgeons too much shit okay?"

That made me laugh and roll my eyes. "I'll try but no promises."

Jeremy then came over to hug me, giving me a smile. "Just think about all the new Saturday morning friend dates we're going to have."

Since Jeremy and I had gotten closer, we started watching cooking shows Saturday morning together. We even started to cook together and sometimes they turned out like shit but sometimes we actually followed the recipes perfectly. It started to become a tradition and was something I looked forward to. Sometimes we pushed it off to a different day, but we always cooked or baked together once a week. He'd become like a brother to me.

"I can't wait."

My eyes didn't start to water until Porter's face came into view. Before he could say anything I wrapped my arms around his neck in a hug. He hugged me back, lightly kissing my neck. "What if something happens," I cried into his shirt.

"Absolutely nothing will," he said while tightening his hold on me. He then pulled back to look into my eyes. "The only thing that's going to happen is you're going to come out being one hundred percent Levi. That's pretty spectacular, don't you think?"

"Yeah," I said in between sobs. "It is."

He wiped all of the tears off of my cheeks before kissing me. "I'll see you very soon darlin'. I love you so much."

"I love you Porter."

The nurse was then wheeling me towards the operating room, my hands starting to shake. It took a little bit longer before I was finally ready to go, lying on a table with a lot of doctors and nurses. The anesthesiologist next to me noticed my shaking hands, giving them a firm squeeze.

"Everything is going to be okay Levi," she said with a smile.

"Thank you," I said with a shaky breath. "Hey doc, while you're down there do you want to make my butt a lot bigger?"

The doctors simply laughed, the atmosphere feeling lighter in the room now. If something were to happen at least I'd go out in my signature flare. I then watched as the anesthesiologist put the anesthesia mask on my face, giving me another warm smile.

"Okay Levi we're going to count back from ten okay? I want you to count with me."

"Ten."

"Nine."

"Eight."

My eyes were shut and the world disappeared before I could count to seven.

****

The next time my eyes opened, I thought I was dead. The room was dark and so quiet I thought I was alone, until my heavy eyes looked over to see a familiar body next to the bed. My head and body hurt too much to try and see who it was before my eyes were shutting again.

****

The second time my eyes opened my entire body felt like it was on fire. A weird sound came from my mouth as my eyes finally focused on the surroundings around me. I was in a room, the world was dark outside the window, it was still dark, and I was in fucking pain.

A hand was then being placed on my hand, making me slowly turn my head. Even though my eyes were really tired I recognized Porter's worried face. "Levi?" He asked, as my eyes were feeling heavy again. "Are you hurting?"

My hand weakly gripped onto his as my eyes tightly shut. "It hurts so bad," I cried.

"I know," he whispered as he rested his head against mine. "I know Levi, but you're doing great."

"I'm not dead?"

He softly chuckled as I opened my eyes again. "You think I'd let you leave me that easily?" His fingers gently roamed over my cheek. "Your surgery went well, really well. Does it feel like your pain meds are wearing off?"

"I think so."

Porter was then doing something on the side of the bed, my eyes getting too heavy to focus. Right as the nurse walked in I noticed something on Porter's arm, was that a bandage?

"...everything.... okay..... pain...... worse..... feel...... better."

I was falling in and out of consciousness as the nurse said whatever it was she was saying. I barely registered her doing something to the IV in my arm, Porter still besides me.

"You're not leaving right?" I whispered while grabbing his arm.

"They'd have to drag me out of here. I'll be here for you, always." Thank god I heard all of what he said.

With that my eyes shut and I once again slipped into the darkness.

****

By the time my eyes opened again I was feeling slightly better. Not by much, I mean I was still in excruciating fucking pain. But going through this and feeling this kind of pain was worth it. I was going to finally be able to look at myself and not hate every single thing I saw. My eyes blinked multiple times before looking over and seeing Porter sitting next to my bed. He had dark circles under his eyes and looked worried until he looked at my eyes. His entire face lit up as he smiled.

"Hey," he whispered while his fingers were slowly running over my arm. "Do you need the nurse?"

"Not right now," my hoarse voice said. I finally looked down at the sheet covering my body before looking back over at Porter. "Can I see?"

"Let me get the doctor," he said while pressing something I couldn't see. "I'd rather have him move the bandages; I don't want to hurt you."

A few minutes later the doctor was coming into the room, a nurse with him. "Hi Levi, nice to see you up. I was here a little bit ago but you were still a little groggy from the anesthesia." I watched him put some gloves on before moving closer to me. "Your surgery was excellent. We were all really pleased with how everything turned out. Ready to see?"

"Yes, please."

I watched as the nurse pulled back the blanket and gown, the doctor removing the bandages a little. He couldn't take it off all the way but he moved it enough where I could see everything. The sight was so overwhelming I started to sob while staring at myself.

"This is actually me?"

"It sure is," the doctor said. "This is really you Levi. Now don't worry, I know it might look a little rough right now but it'll look better with time. This will take around six to eight weeks to heal so please don't do any strenuous activity for a while."

"Thank you," I sobbed again as I continued to look at myself. "Thank you for finally helping me."

He smiled, his eyes looking tired but hopeful. "Of course Levi, that's what I'm here for. I'm here to help everyone look and feel how they truly are. Now, you're going to have to stay here for at least three days. I need to make sure everything is going well before you go home. We have you on a pretty strong pain killer right now but if something doesn't feel right call the nurse okay? If something is truly off I'll come in and make sure everything still looks good. But how you look right now is very promising."

He then gently covered me again, the nurse tucking everything back in. We all talked for a little while longer before they left and it was just Porter and I again. His fingers slowly and gently touched my cheek before kissing my forehead.

"How long was it?" I asked.

"Almost five hours. Longest five hours of my life."

"You stayed here the whole time?"

He gave me a look before asking, "Where else would I go, Disney World? The man I loved was getting very complicated and risky surgery, I was going to be here. The only time I wasn't was when they were prepping you for surgery but I was here the whole other time."

My eyes traveled down to his arm where a bandage was sticking out from under his shirt. "Does this have anything to do with you leaving?"

"It is," he said.

"Can I see?"

He nodded before removing the bandage a little so I could see his other tattoos. Except now there was a third roman numeral underneath the other two, his dad and Kurt's birthday.

"I set this up a while ago because I wanted it to take as little time as possible. And I didn't want to leave you after at all; I'm going to be here to help you during recovery. But the artist, Chuck, is an old friend of mine and luckily his shop isn't far from here at all. I went in and came out lickety split. I now have the three most important men on my arm."

"Wait," I said while looking at the ink. "This is my birthday?" My eyes welled with tears as I gently pulled his shirt and kissed him. "I love you so much."

"And I love you Levi, with my entire heart." The pain was making it difficult to focus too much longer, Porter noticing. "Try to get some sleep darlin', I'll be here when you wake up."

He didn't have to tell me twice. Before I knew it I was slipping back into sleep. But this time I knew I was going to come out of the darkness just fine.

*

The next day Porter was still being stubborn about leaving to take a break. "Why don't you go eat something? You look exhausted."

"I'm fine Levi," he said with a smile. "I'm not leaving you."

"It's not like I'm going anywhere. I'd feel better if you just ate a bagel or something."

Wyatt and Jeremy had just left, Porter not even wanting to eat the snacks they brought for him. He was probably sick of just sitting here staring at me anyway. I mean I know I was a sight to see but right now I was a little rough around the edges.

"I'm not even hungry."

Right as he said that I could hear his stomach growling, him giving me a sheepish look. "Looks like you're busted. Please just go to the cafeteria and get something to eat. Please? For me?"

He smiled before kissing me. "Not fair when you look at me like that darlin'. Fine, but I'll be back in a few minutes okay?"

"Porter," I said while intertwining our fingers together. "I'm okay, I really am. I don't want you to be bored out of your mind here, if there's something you need to go do you can."

He simply gave me a look while shaking his head, kissing my hand. "No way would I do that Levi."

"I know you're not just going to abandon me here silly. And I don't want you getting too hungry. And if you start stinking up this room from body odor from not showering I'm going to have to send you away."

With that he laughed, his shoulders shaking. "Alright, alright. I'll go grab something really fast and be right back."

"No, don't rush!"

"Fine," he huffed while getting up. He left a kiss on top of my head as he said, "I love you."

"I'll love you more if you actually eat and don't rush."

He laughed again, giving me a salute before leaving the room. Once the door was shut I closed my eyes after yawning. This was probably a perfect time to get some sleep, plus, my bottom half was starting to hurt again. Just as I was about to drift off to sleep I heard the door open again, making me chuckle.

"That didn't last very long."

"Alexis!"

My entire body went rigged as I opened my eyes to see none other than my mother standing in the doorway, looking pissed.

Seventeen

L^{evi}

"Wh... what are you doing here?" I asked while watching her come into the room. My hands gripped the sheets when she shut the door behind her. She was then rushing over to the bed as her eyes stared down at the sheet covering my body.

"Look what they've done to you," she said while shaking her head. "Don't worry honey; we'll sue all of these people." I then watched, in horror, as she moved closer to me before lifting the sheet up. Her face went white as she saw the bandage.

"No, stop!" I practically yelled as she pulled the bandage back and gasped.

I wanted to shove her off of me; I didn't want her seeing me. "How dare they do this to you, we'll get this taken care of."

"Stop!" My cracked voice said as I shoved her hands off of me and throwing the sheet over myself, making sure the bandage was back on. "Why are you here?"

"I got a letter in the mail, some insurance document, but it was addressed to you. Even though it didn't say the gorgeous name I gave you when you were born. The letter was talking about some ridiculous surgery so I came out here as quick as I could."

My heartbeat was going wild as I stared at her. I thought I had changed my address to the ranch but something must've gone to New York. "Why would you come here?"

She gave me a look before putting her hand on top of my groin area, pain erupting all over my body. "I knew you'd probably still be in this little phase and came to bring you home. You're obviously not thinking straight, this country air always changes people. We'll have a doctor turn you back into my little princess."

"Stop it!" I shoved her hand off of me as angry tears slid down my cheeks. "This is not some phase Mom, this is my life! This is how I've always been inside my mind. I've never been the person you thought I've been."

"They must have you on some strong pills Alexis." My body flinched like she slapped me, god I hated that name. "Don't worry honey, we'll get this all situated. Once we get home we can go get manicures and get our hair done, your hair will need to grow out some. You look like a tomboy right now and no one wants that. Oh! Do you remember Dillion Springs? I think you two would be perfect together."

"Stop!" I cried while putting my hands over my face.

"Oh Alexis, you were always such a drama queen."

"I'm Levi."

This time she laughed before petting my hair. "Alexis, this isn't funny anymore. God honey are you even wearing a bra?" My hands dug into my hair as I felt her suddenly touch my chest. I never told her that Wyatt paid for my top surgery, or that I even had one. I tried to keep a lot hidden from her. I even wore hoodies all the time so she wouldn't actually see my chest. "We'll have a plastic surgeon fix these too. You can't be a good wife looking like this. So stop crying Alexis and woman up."

"What the fuck did you just say?"

My hands slid from my face to see Porter standing in the doorway. I hadn't even heard the door open but I was so happy to see him. I've also never seen someone look so incredibly pissed while holding a banana and a sandwich. My mother turned towards him before putting her hands onto her hips.

"Don't you country hicks have any class? You don't curse when women are present."

"There's only one bitch in this fucking room, no women."

She gasped before putting her hand onto her chest. "And who exactly do you think you are?"

"I'm Levi's boyfriend."

She visibly flinched before smoothing down her top. "I don't know who that is. I'm here for my daughter Alexis. Beautiful girl, such a shame she's turned into this. But I'm taking her back to New York and we'll sort everything out."

Porter dry laughed as he stared at her. "I take that back, you're not a bitch. You're a fucking cunt."

"How dare you say that to me!"

"How dare you talk about Levi like he isn't even in the fucking room!"

Since they were both shouting now a security guard was walking over before stepping into the room. "Is everything okay in here?"

"No, it isn't. She needs to leave," Porter said.

"I'm not leaving without my daughter Alexis!"

"STOP!" I finally screamed at her, making her turn towards me. "I've never been your daughter. I'm not a woman, I'm a man. My name is Levi."

I watched as she then lowered down to my level before practically spitting in my face, "Alexis."

With that Porter grabbed her before the security guard could, making her scream at him. The security guard took over as she was then being escorted out of the room, more guards coming over.

"You'll never be a real man Alexis. You were born with breasts and a vagina, no amount of surgery will ever make you-" Porter slammed the door before she could say more.

My entire body was shaking as I started to violently cry, Porter instantly coming over. I was crying so hard I felt that awful feeling of going to throw up, which luckily Porter realized. Probably because I was gagging on my tears but luckily I didn't puke on myself. He brought the trash can over just in time so I could empty what little I had in my stomach. I cried so hard I kept puking, until I was just dry heaving. Porter's hand was gently rubbing my back as the door opened and my body went rigid again.

Luckily it was just a nurse who heard the commotion and wanted to make sure I was okay. I had no idea what Porter said to her, my puking sounds were drowning everything out. But when there were no more tears left in me I pulled back from the gross trash can. I watched as Porter was then wiping a warm wash cloth over my mouth before moving the trash can onto the floor.

He was then leaving soft kisses all over my face before saying, "I've not going to talk about her for a long time because she isn't worth the oxygen. I know you know what she said wasn't true; she was trying to get under your skin. God, I don't know how you put up with her growing up." He took a deep breath before kissing my knuckles. "You have no idea how bad I wanted to punch her. But she seemed like the kind who would press charges and shit, I didn't want to deal with that. The fucking nerve of some people." He took another deep breath before saying, "I'm so sorry someone said such evil and vile things to you. Did she do anything physical to you?"

"She grabbed my bandage really hard. I don't know if it did anything but it really hurts." He quickly pushed the nurse button before leaning his head against mine. "Don't get too close, I smell like vomit."

"First off, I wouldn't care if you were covered in actual shit or literally anything else. Nothing would ever make me not get close to you." He took another shaky breath before saying, "I'll spend the rest of my life making you feel the exact opposite of her. I want you to know how loved you are, so fucking loved Levi."

I started sobbing again as he kissed my nose as the nurse came in. She checked on everything and luckily nothing seemed to be abnormal. She was almost more distraught than I was, her pretty eyes filled with tears. She left and came back with an armful of cookies. "I took these from our breakroom, if there's anything else you need please let me know."

When she was gone Porter helped me brush my teeth on the bed, mainly because I couldn't handle how my teeth felt. He was so attentive it was making me cry again, my arms wrapping around him. He climbed onto the bed besides me, making sure to not hurt me. His giant body was curled next to me, the even feel of his heartbeat hitting my shoulder as he lay on his side.

My fingers dug into his arm as my eyes suddenly got too heavy to stay open. The one thing that was making me feel better was knowing I would wake up to Porter and he'd be here the rest of my life. And I'd never have to see that devil again.

**

"I can't believe this; I'm actually going to kill her." Wyatt was angrily pacing by the foot of my bed as Jeremy and Kurt sat on my right side. Porter was still on my left side, really helping to calm me down.

"She's not worth the time," Porter said. "Trust me; I should be in jail right now."

"I never knew how evil she really was," Kurt said as a deep frown covered his face. "Levi, why didn't you say anything when you were younger?"

The look he was giving me was making me feel guilty as I said, "I'm sorry Kurt. I couldn't leave Wyatt; he was the only support system I had. And she only started getting nasty when I was discovering the real me. And plus I'm not sure if you knew but I'm more of a city guy." That finally made him smile as Porter chuckled next to me.

"I'd say you're turning a little more country day by day."

I looked up into his eyes while saying, "I'm still not wearing cowboy boots."

He laughed before kissing my head. Before he could respond a knock came from the door. "Come in," Porter said as we all turned, expecting a nurse or a doctor.

Instead it was a group of people walking in, all seeming really happy and bubbly. "Good afternoon!" One woman around my age said with a wave. "We're from the Cedar Rapids community theatre going around and singing some of the newest songs from our upcoming musical. Would you all like to hear a song or would you like us to leave?"

Everyone looked at me before I instantly nodded. "Please stay."

The woman smiled before they all started singing, their voices sounding so nice together. They performed a few songs before moving on to a different room, giving another wave before they left. I had always been interested in theatre growing up but never knew what to do or how to pursue it. I'd been too focused on myself to even try and find something I liked as a hobby. But now I was actually starting to think about the future.

For so long I had only thought of how in the hell I was going to get to where I wanted to be physically, I never thought of anything else. Now I could actually explore the interests I had growing up but was too chicken to do. Now I could actually start... living. As my true self, and not completely hate myself every time I looked at myself in the mirror. Now I actually had a family who loved me, not the version of myself my mother had in her head.

"Hey," Porter's gentle voice said next to me. I hadn't even realized I was crying until he wiped my cheeks off. "What's wrong?"

"Nothing," I said with a smile. "I'm just really happy."

He smiled too as his thumb slowly ran over my skin. "Happy looks amazing on you."

I then pulled him down towards me so I could whisper into his ear. "I'll also look amazing once I can ride on you again."

He groaned before saying, "You can't say stuff like that darlin'. I'm going to be hard twenty four seven just imagining you like that."

"Think you can wait eight weeks?"

"I'd wait eighty years for you."

That brought more tears to my eyes as I said, "I love you."

"I love you."

My face buried into his neck as I listened to Wyatt, Jeremy and Kurt talking about something, their laughter filling the room. I don't know how I got so lucky.

Jeremy

My eyes wandered over to Wyatt sitting next to me on the couch, the dogs by our feet. It'd been a stressful day ever since Levi told us what his mother told him. I wouldn't even call her a mother though, so not quite sure what to call her. Wyatt and Porter had some choice words for her alright, all things she deserved. I was really happy that Levi wouldn't have to deal with her bullshit anymore.

Once we left the hospital we grabbed some food before driving back home. Levi would get to come home in two days, since the doctor wanted him to stay an extra night. But as my eyes lingered over Wyatt again I thought about how no one else would be here for a little bit. My palms started to sweat nervously as I forced myself to stare back at the TV.

One thing that Wyatt is is patient. He hasn't tried to rush anything between us, especially physically. I felt bad in a way because the only thing we've done is kiss and cuddle. And while I loved that, I know he would probably like to do a little more. It was scary thinking about doing something really intimate with someone but there's no one else I'd rather open myself up to like that.

Before I could do anything he suddenly stood up while saying, "Want another Coke?"

Since I was too chicken to say I only wanted him, I nodded and watched him walk into the kitchen. Before chickening out again I stood up and walked into the next room, seeing his back as he poured drinks by the sink. Taking a deep breath and giving myself a small pep talk, I walked over before I was behind him. My hands then gently landed onto his back, my fingers burying into the soft fabric of his shirt. He then slowly turned around which made my fingers slowly run over his stomach. I wanted him to feel so good, I just wasn't sure if I could actually do it.

Before he could say anything I whispered, "Please kiss me."

My heart sped up as he leaned closer to me, he could probably hear how loud it was beating. Once his lips landed onto mine I wrapped my arms around his neck before burying my fingers into his hair. His long arms wrapped around me and pulled me up against him, where I could feel him getting hard.

When his lips slowly moved to my neck I managed to shakily say, "Wyatt."

He pulled back and looked down into my eyes. "Are you okay?"

"Yeah," I said while feeling my cheeks heat up. "I was uhm... wondering if I could... I mean if we both could... do things? Erm to each other I mean. Sexually."

I knew my cheeks were lit up as he seemed to stare into my soul. "Are you sure you're ready?"

"I know we've only kissed and it probably hasn't been that fun for you."

His hands landed onto my cheeks, my hands wrapping around his wrists. "I'd never push you to do anything Jeremy. I know I'm more experienced in this department and didn't want you to think sex was all I wanted out of you. And kissing you is always going to be fun, always. But please don't think that this is something we need to do just because Levi and Porter aren't here."

"It's not just that," I said. "I feel really safe with you."

He stared at me for a few seconds before kissing my forehead. "I wish I would have waited for you."

"You're here now though. That's all I care about."

"You're unreal," he said before lightly kissing me again.

With that he grabbed my hand and walked upstairs to his room, gently shutting the door behind him. Suddenly I was getting super nervous realizing this was the first man who was going to see such a vulnerable side of me. All of my insecurities were hitting me square in the face and the fear that he would turn out to be like the only other person I had given my heart to.

"Hey," he said while putting his hands onto my face. "Where did you go- are you okay? It's okay if you changed your mind about-"

"I want babies," I suddenly blurted out. His dark eyebrows rose as I continued to word vomit. "I want to get married one day and have at least three kids." My heart was beating even faster now. "I'm sorry; I know that's not a turn on. And I don't know why I'm saying this. I just... I didn't want to give myself to someone without that being out there. I'm not into casual things, I want something longer." Embarrassed tears were stinging my eyes as I looked down. "That was stupid and I ruined the mood I'm sorry. I was hoping my stupid insecurities would have gone away by now."

"That wasn't stupid at all," he said gently. "Can I see your eyes Jeremy?" When I finally looked back up he was smiling. "My plan was to never get you naked then simply leave. You're the person I've been waiting my entire life for Jer, you don't have to worry about me taking off. I've thought of our future plenty of times, I just didn't want to freak you out or make you think I was trying to rush things. I'm here to stay. And besides, you are the owner of my heart. There's no other place I'd want to be." I wrapped my arms around him in a tight hug. "I want babies too," he whispered against my neck. "And plus, I'm in love with you."

That made me pull back and stare up at him. My eyes watered as his thumbs caught all the tears that fell from my eyes. "I'm in love with you too Wyatt."

A pretty smile lit up his face as he connected our lips again before gently lifting me into his arms. My legs wrapped around his waist as he walked over towards the bed and gently lowered me onto it.

"Still want to start learning each other physically, love?"

My heart about exploded when he called me that. "I do."

With wide eyes I watched as he slowly took his shirt off before letting the fabric drop to the floor. My hands instantly wandered over his pecs before I took my shirt off too. His dark eyes were roaming all over my chest before he leaned down to kiss my skin. When his mouth ended up onto one of my nipples the feeling was enough to undue me, I wasn't going to last long. His mouth was making me arch my back and moan from the feeling. He then kissed down my chest and stomach before he actually started nuzzling my pants. My cheeks were on fire as I gasped and practically pulled him back up to me.

As our mouths met again he slowly rolled our hips together, the feeling making me pull back to cry out. We both still had our pants on but feeling his erection through his pants was such an exciting feeling. I couldn't even imagine what it would feel like when we were naked up against each other.

"Is it okay if I take my pants off?" He asked.

After a nervous swallow I whispered, "Yes."

I then watched as he pulled back to slip out of his pants, leaving him in a pair of dark blue boxers. The color looked really nice against his skin. Before he could ask if I wanted mine off I slowly slid my pants off, chucking them onto the floor. His mouth then lowered back down onto mine, one hand slowly running up and down my leg. I had to pull back when our boxers rubbed up against each other's, my entire body tingling. I wanted to be closer to him before I came like an overexcited teenager.

"Wyatt," I panted as his dark eyes found mine. "Can these come off?"

"Of course love," he whispered.

He then slowly slid his boxers off first, my fingers digging into the sheets when I finally saw him. "It's not fair," I said, not realizing I said that out loud before seeing the confused look on his face.

"What isn't fair?"

"That you look like you were sculpted out of stone or something."

"Have you not looked in the mirror?" He asked while running his fingers softly over my cheeks. "Ever since we met I have been floored by your beauty. You're stunning Jeremy, you're like a cowboy sculpted out of stone. I mean have you seen...." He then lowered his head down towards my stomach before running his tongue over my skin. "These abs?" I couldn't help but shiver as he kissed me. "You're the most beautiful person inside and out I've ever met."

When he moved back up towards the bed I wrapped my arms around his neck, lowering our mouths together again. "Thank you," I whispered when we pulled back. "You're so nice."

"I speak the truth love."

That made me shimmy my boxers down, Wyatt helping before they were tossed onto the floor. "So gorgeous," he whispered before slowly grabbing onto me and making me cry out. No one else had ever touched me let alone seen me naked, and I was so glad it was Wyatt.

The way his hand was running over me was basically making me see stars, but I didn't want to be the only one feeling good. I hesitantly gripped onto him, my fingers running over his thickness and veins. As our hands were running over each other I suddenly wanted more. I wanted to know what it would be like to taste him, if he tasted me.

"Can we try mouths?" I whispered while feeling my cheeks heat up.

"Of course," he said after giving me a soft kiss on the mouth.

Before I could move he was slowly sliding down my body, leaving kisses all over my skin. The next thing I knew he was taking me into his mouth and making me cry out at the feeling. My fingers started shaking as I dug them into his hair as the feeling of his tongue on me was making my hips arch off the bed. I knew I wasn't going to last long but I already was feeling the tingling in my toes.

"Wyatt," I cried as he took more of my length into his mouth. His fingers were slowly running over my thighs as my legs wrapped around his back. "Wait," I said while the tingling started getting more intense. "I..."

It was too late to try and warn him because the next thing I knew my entire body was shaking. His mouth stayed on me the entire time and swallowed everything, his dark eyes finding mine. When he pulled back I was breathing heavily as he crawled up the bed and slowly kissed me.

"I'm sorry," I whispered. "I definitely thought I'd last a little longer."

"Don't apologize," he said while running his fingers over my cheek. "You're perfect in every way Jeremy."

"So are you," I whispered as we kissed again. This time I could really taste myself on him and... it was such a strange and intoxicating taste. I suddenly had an urge to taste him, and have his taste on my tongue.

That made me pull back and shove him onto his back before nervously moving down his body. I ran a shaky hand over his length before leaning down and giving a soft kiss to the side of him. One of his large hands ended up in my hair as he deeply moaned above me. At least I was making him feel good. But I wanted him to feel better.

After a shaky breath I opened my mouth and wrapped my lips around him. I tried to remember everything that he had just done on me, which was amazing. Okay, I can do this. I slowly bobbed my head up and down on him while trying to get more of him into my mouth. I wasn't really sure what to do with my hands so I wrapped one of them on the bottom of his length. I kept my other hand on his thigh like he did with me.

After getting the courage to look up at him I felt my entire body erupt into a blush when I realized he was already looking at me. "Fuck," he deeply groaned as his fingers tightened into my hair. I could tell he was getting close before suddenly an intense taste was in my mouth. Wyatt was breathing heavily as his fingers massaged my hair before I pulled back, trying to swallow all of it. When I finally did he pulled me back up towards him, his mouth leaving kisses all over my face.

"Guess I didn't last long either," he said with a smile. "I've just been envisioning this for so long and you're sexy as hell. There is one thing I do want to see, is it okay if I turn you over for a second?"

"Okay," I said as his hands turned me onto my stomach. I wasn't sure what he wanted, but I guess to see my ass. His lips were right over where my tattoo was, realization hitting me.

"I've also been envisioning what this tattoo looks like," he said against my skin. "So beautiful." He then slowly turned me back over with a smile on his face. "Are you okay?"

I nodded before yawning. "Really okay. Just tired."

"Before you fall asleep let's go clean up a little love."

He helped me off the bed and picked me up in his arms to walk to the bathroom. When our bodies and teeth were clean we ended back up in bed, after putting some pajamas on. His long arms wrapped around me as I contently sighed and buried my face under his neck.

"I love you so much Wyatt, I'm so glad you and Levi came here."

"I love you too Jeremy," he whispered into my ear. "Coming here was the best thing we've ever done. You've changed my life for the better."

My arms tightened around him as he pulled the blankets up closer around us. I couldn't wait to spend the rest of my nights like this, wrapped up in the arms of the man I loved. I never thought I would get to find love like this, I never thought I'd be this happy. I don't know what I did to have love not only for me but for Porter as well, but I was never letting it go.

Eighteen

L^{evi}

"Have a good Christmas Levi!"

"Thanks guys, you too!"

After our goodbye hugs I jogged to the front door, smiling when I saw Porter's truck waiting outside. I still loved that he offered to drive to my rehearsals once the weather started to get bad. The snow here was no joke and he wanted to make sure I got there safely.

It'd been about six months since I had surgery and was finally to the point where I could wake up with no pain. For the most part I'd been waking up in pain almost every single day, which is annoying as fuck. But it was all worth it since I was able to finally be one hundred percent myself. I had to go through physical therapy, still having multiple sessions booked. Once my therapist cleared me for some more activity, I looked into theatre. The actors and actresses that came to my room when I was still in the hospital really inspired me. I wanted to do the things I've always wanted, just didn't know how. So once I was feeling up to it I drove to the theatre and auditioned.

There I've met some of my closest friends, people I truly cherish in my life. Having friends that truly loved and respected the real me was still odd to me, but I couldn't be happier. There was nothing more I loved than performing with all of them, besides being at the farm of course. And now that the final play of the year was over, I could relax with Porter at home. Lounging around on the couch with him had become truly one of my favorite things.

Adjusting the hat on my head I carefully made my way over towards his truck before diving into the warmth inside. "Hey darlin'," he said while leaning over to kiss me. "How was everyone?"

"They were good," I said while shivering. He turned the heat up while starting to pull away from the curb. "Look what Kaci got me!" I held up a pair of mittens that were a soft mint green. "She made these aren't they soft?" I gently rubbed them against his stubbly face as he laughed. "Oh and Tommy got me this blanket," I said while digging into my bagful of goodies before pulling out a white fluffy blanket with rainbows over it. "Jack got everyone books from this cool bookstore he found and Penny got me a gigantic coffee mug."

"Sounds like the part went well," he said with a smile. "I'm glad you had a good time."

"It was so fun! And we had some food delivered from that bomb ass pizza place you and I went to that one time. I feel like I have a food baby," I said while placing my hands onto my stomach.

Porter gently laughed again before merging onto the highway as snowflakes started to fall. "Hopefully you aren't too full for some dessert."

"You know I'm always down for that."

I then turned the Christmas songs playing on the radio up higher before singing along to the songs. I'd been so happy lately, even doing small things like making dinner made me feel like I actually belonged. Having friends and family that love and appreciate you will make you feel like that.

By the time we pulled into the ranch it was full on snowing, looking like a snow globe. Porter parked his truck next to Wyatt's SUV in the driveway before we both got out. Right as I started walking up the steps I felt something pelt my back, making me turn to see a laughing Porter.

"So it's like that huh?" I asked while grabbing some snow and rolled it into a ball.

"Looks like it city boy."

With a laugh I threw the snowball at him, hitting him on the coat. By the time he picked up more snow I was already running away, both of us laughing. We pelted each other with snow before his long arms were wrapping around me. We eventually landed onto the snow covered ground, his larger body hovering over mine.

He leaned down to gently kiss me, my arms wrapping around his neck. Once he leaned back he stared at me for a couple of moments, making me raise one eyebrow. "What? Upset that I whooped your ass with snow?"

"I was just thinking how great it looks on you."

"Winning? Yeah, I am a great winner."

"I meant happiness."

That made instant butterflies fly into my stomach before pulling him closer to me. "Porter you can't say stuff like that," I muttered into his coat.

"Why not?" He laughed. "I'm able to compliment my boyfriend."

"I know but you know that kind of stuff makes me cry. And I cry too much."

With that he pulled back slightly so I could see his eyes. His hands then gently rested onto my cheeks as more snow was coming down around us. "You don't cry too much Levi, not at all. The fact that no one told you things like that growing up makes me want to cry. And you deserve literally all the happiness in the world, for the rest of your life. And I can't wait to do things that cause that happiness, like just lying in the snow."

I smiled, pulling him down to kiss again. "Happiness looks good on you too," I whispered into his ear.

"Hey you dweebs."

We both looked up to see Wyatt standing on the porch, giving us both a look. "What?" I sassily asked. "Can't you see we're busy being all cute and shit?"

Wyatt rolled his eyes, a small smile on his face. "Why don't you come inside to be all cute and shit? I don't want you two getting sick for Christmas because you were idiots and lying out in the snow."

"Whatever," I said as Porter laughed.

He then helped me up, grabbing my bags before walking into the warm house. "There are you happy now?"

Jeremy started snickering from the stove where he was stirring what looked like soup when Porter and I walked into the kitchen. "I'd be pissed if you got sick for the first real family Christmas we're having. Theo, Marie and Katie are coming for Christmas."

"I know," I said while plopping down into a chair. "But that isn't for two days."

"Enough time to get sick."

"Everything will be okay honey," Jeremy said while coming over to where Wyatt was sitting. He wrapped his arms around his neck, Wyatt instantly calming down. "Porter is built like a steel trap and Levi is one of the toughest guys I know."

Wyatt smiled when Jeremy kissed his cheek, those two looking so cute I wanted to vomit. "I know, I'm just nervous."

"Yeah that's pretty obvious," I muttered before he threw a napkin at me. I laughed, his own echoing mine. "Kurt and Debbie are coming over too."

It wasn't that big of a surprise when Kurt and Debbie started to date after he was discharged from the hospital. She was honestly like a mother to me, she was so nice and thoughtful. Her and Marie were like the mothers I always wanted, and now I had two. My actual mother was served with a restraining order after what she did to me in the hospital. I hoped I never saw her again in my life.

"Does this mean you're going to be a pain in the ass until Christmas is over?" I asked.

"Sorry for wanting our house to look good for our family."

That sentence made all the snark instantly leave my body. The fact that we had an actual home, together, with the love of our lives was already perfect. And then the fact that we have actual family this year, was still wild to me.

"Levi?" Porter's voice asked from beside me. "Are you okay?"

"You know I was only teasing you Lev," Wyatt said.

"No I know," I said while gripping onto Porter's hand. "It's just, we have family now." Porter squeezed my hand while Wyatt nodded. "It won't just be us for Christmas eating frozen dinners by our tiny tree."

Wyatt reached across the table for my other hand before saying, "And we'll never be alone again Lev."

Jeremy came over to give me a gigantic bear hug before wiping his eyes. He then moved back over to the stove and stirred the soup. "You guys are making me cry like I just watched one of those Christmas movies."

"God those movies all have the same plot," Porter said.

"No they don't!" Jeremy said after walking back over to the table.

"Oh geez here we go," Wyatt said as I started laughing. "Before they start bickering why don't you take your twin." He then stood up and lifted Jeremy into his arms, Jeremy's laugh echoing throughout the kitchen. "And I'll take mine."

"I need to turn off the stove!"

I laughed when Wyatt walked over and turned it off, Jeremy still giggling in his arms. I started pretend gagging when they were kissing, pulling Porter up from the table. "Okay have fun with that, we'll eat soup once you guys are done humping it up in here."

"Oh my god we are not!" Jeremy said before loudly laughing.

Porter laughed while swinging his arm over my shoulder before leaving the kitchen. Before I could start walking up the stairs he placed my bags onto the steps and pulled me towards the door. "Where are we going?"

"Just one final pit stop before we eat," he said while placing my hat back on and helping to zip my coat up. "That okay?"

"Fine with me, as long as I don't have to see those two love birds be all cutesy."

Porter simply gave me a smile before grabbing my hand. "I know you actually love seeing them together."

"Ugh fine you're right."

"Like always."

He laughed when I jumped on his back, his arms immediately securing me to his body. "I think you're thinking of me always being right."

"You are always right," he said with a smile.

We walked in a comfortable silence for a few moments before he turned the corner by the barn. I gasped while seeing his horse Ace hooked up to a carriage covered in Christmas lights.

"What in the actual fuck?" I asked. "You did not."

He carefully set me down as we got int front of Ace, who was boredly looking between us. "Is this okay?"

"Oh my god Porter!" I cried while wrapping him in a hug. "I can't believe this! This is beautiful!"

Porter smiled while snowflakes dusted his hair. "Seeing that smile on your face is worth everything to me."

With that he gave me a long kiss, the kind that made my toes curl. He then helped me into the carriage before untying Ace. He then got into the carriage next to me, pulling a blanket over our laps. My arms wrapped around his as we started to move across the property. "And you say you don't watch those cheesy romance movies."

He looked over at me, his smile shining. "I may have seen the end of one Jer was watching. And I'll be cheesy for you any day."

"I love cheese," I said while resting my head against his shoulder.

We rode around in comfortable silence until he wrapped his arm around me, making me look up at him. "Merry Christmas Levi, I love you."

Tears were running down my face as he kissed me, snowflakes falling onto our faces. "Merry Christmas Porter, you're the best present I could have ever wished for. I love you."

With that I pulled Christmas music up on my phone, both of us singing along to the songs. I definitely knew that once we went back inside we were for sure watching the cheesiest of Christmas movies. But until then, I'd enjoy this actual romance movie taking place right now. One I never thought would exist for someone like me. Who knew that Iowa would be the place that I would find love and my true self. As I stared up at Porter's laughing face, I couldn't imagine being anywhere else.

Wyatt

"I don't know how you're such a good cook," I said after finishing the soup. Jeremy's famous blush covered his cheeks, making me smile. It didn't matter if we had been together six months, he still blushed at every compliment. His blushes were deeper when we were in bed exploring each other's bodies, something I craved. Everything about him turned me on and I couldn't possibly love him more.

I knew that Levi and Porter were currently out in the carriage, something that I knew Levi would love. He loved horses now, especially Ace. He was even out riding more with Porter, he'd never admit it but he was turning into a real cowboy. Porter even got him to wear cowboy boots, something he always said he would never wear. But love makes you do crazy things.

I was thinking the same thing as I looked over at Jeremy across the table. "It's just soup," he said while getting up and taking the bowls to the sink.

Once he started rinsing the bowls I got up and wrapped my arms around him, his body automatically leaning back into mine. "It's not just soup,"

I said while kissing his neck. "You put love into everything you do and I admire that about you." I kissed his neck again before taking the bowls from him and rinsing them, putting them into the dishwasher. I then grabbed his hand before saying, "Come on, let's go watch a movie."

We walked up to our room, closing the door once we were both inside. It was still pretty light outside but the lights in the room twinkled when Jeremy turned them on. He had strung lights on our headboard and basically all over the room, giving the room a nice glow.

I had found out Jeremy really liked decorating for holidays, especially Christmas. The four of us had fun decorating the house and setting up the tree, it was nice to see the twins and Levi get so excited. Especially since Levi never got excited for any holiday anymore, but now his eyes lit up and he had a real smile.

My own smile came from the man sitting on the bed, currently flipping through movies. After climbing next to him he asked, "What kind of movie do you want?"

"Anything is fine with me."

"So you're saying another cheesy Christmas movie?"

I couldn't help but laugh before saying, "Whatever you'd like love."

I then pulled the blankets around us as he snuggled up against me. The movie was cheesy, just the way Jeremy liked them. But I wouldn't have it any other way. When the movie was done and another one started playing, I had planned on getting up to change into pajamas when Jeremy's hand touched my thigh. I simply figured he was readjusting but his fingers were slowly running over my jean clad thigh.

Before I could say anything he slowly sat up, those big innocent eyes staring at me. He then leaned forward and kissed me, my arms wrapping around him. He readjusted himself so he was straddling me, already turning me on. He then pulled back to stare at me, so many emotions splashing across his face.

"Are you okay?" I whispered while gently running my hand over his back.

With a shaky breath he said, "I want you to make love to me." A blush instantly covered his cheeks.

"And here I thought you couldn't get any sexier." He smiled, making his body relax a little. "But are you sure?"

He nodded, swallowing loudly. "Please make love to me Wyatt."

I slowly switched our positions so he was underneath my body. "You don't ever have to beg, love."

With that I leaned down and kissed him, his fingers running through my curls. He then tugged at my shirt, making me pull back to whip it off my body. His fingers lightly touched all over my skin, feeling like butterfly kisses. He then took his shirt off as I reconnected our lips and bringing our bodies closer together.

He then gently pushed me onto my back and taking my pants off, making my dick even harder. I fucking loved his new found confidence. "God you're the most beautiful person I've ever seen," I said as he smiled.

"That's how I feel about you. I just want you to feel good."

"I always feel good around you love, always. I can't wait to be inside of you."

That made his eyes widen, his fingers tightening on my stomach. He then took my boxers off and attached his mouth to me, making me see stars. "Fuck," I groaned while gently gripping his hair. I had to tightly grip the side of the bed when my hips tried to thrust into his mouth. "Jesus Jer you're unreal," I groaned again. I was so excited to get my mouth onto him that I was basically shaking, it was crazy what he did to me.

When he pulled back to take a deep breath I pulled him to me, my mouth instantly finding his. My dick was still wet with his saliva as I got him onto his back, quickly taking his pants and boxers off. I then instantly took his entire length into my mouth, making him jump and hold onto my curls. I fucking loved when he held onto me like that, like he was trying not to lose control. I made sure to give the best head I could, loving the sounds he was making.

I then pulled back and made sure his eyes were on me as I slid a finger into my mouth. His pupils were very dilated as I very gently coaxed the wet finger into him, his eyes twisting in pain. "I know love," I said while running my free hand up and down his thigh. "I promise it'll feel better."

"Mhmm," he said while gripping onto the sheets. "Jesus how do people do this."

"I'm going to keep this one in, while you focus on how fucking sexy you look."

Those big eyes looked at me as he said, "Ha yeah real sexy."

"Your beautiful ass is currently accepting one of my fingers, and soon I'll be completely inside of you. You're sexy as hell Jeremy, especially when your ass is completely filled with me."

His breathing got heavier as he stared at me, making me wonder if I went too far. We haven't really delved into dirty talk before. "Sorry if that went too far I-"

"Don't stop," he said as his cheeks lit up with a blush. "I... I liked it."

My eyebrows rose as I smiled. Who knew sweet little innocent Jeremy would enjoy dirty talk. "I'm going to add a second finger then suck that glorious dick again."

I made sure my second finger wasn't dry before adding it, his eyes closing as his back arched off the bed. Jesus Christ. My mouth returned to him as my fingers slowly starting thrusting in and out of him, his heat driving me insane. Just knowing no one else had been inside of him was making me go insane too. Very gently I pulled my fingers out while taking my mouth off of him, reaching for the bedside table. I grabbed the condoms and lube I had in case we ever got this far, his eyes following me.

I then held the condom out to him before saying, "I'd like you to put this on me."

"Really?"

"I'd love your fingers to put it on me."

He held the condom in his hand as he swallowed again. "And then you'll be inside of me with it?"

"I sure will love."

I watched as he opened the wrapper, his fingers slowly putting it on my erection. His fingers lingered for a few seconds longer before I grabbed the lube. His eyes followed me coat my fingers before sliding them back inside of him. He moaned as my fingers stretched him wider, before he grabbed the bottle and coated his own fingers. I then watched as he ran those fingers over the condom, pulling me closer to him. I gently pulled my fingers out before kissing him, slowly spreading his legs wider.

"Remember to breathe normally okay? Try not to clench up." He nodded, his arms wrapping around my neck as I slowly eased into him. His eyes tightly closed as his fingers dug into my skin. "You're amazing."

One of his legs wrapped around my waist as I slid deeper inside of him, both of us moaning. I kissed him again before grabbing his erection, swallowing his moan. My other hand slid down the leg that was wrapped around me, eventually landing onto his ass cheek. His other leg wrapped around me as I started kissing his neck, his fingers slowly running over my back.

My thrusts picked up as I slid completely inside of him, a moan coming out of my mouth. "Wyatt," he softly moaned while wrapping his arms around my neck. His lips were then leaving soft kisses over my neck, before returning to my lips. I slowed my thrusts down before finding those beautiful eyes again.

The love I felt for this man was insane, I felt like our souls were becoming one in this moment. "I love you," I whispered as his eyes grew misty with tears.

"I love you."

It didn't take that much longer for Jeremy to release, his body shaking around mine. Seeing him like that was making the familiar tingle rise throughout my body before feeling myself release as well. He was breathing heavily underneath me as my thrusts slowly stopped. I then gave him a gentle kiss before pulling out of him. He was full on crying when I pulled him into a hug, kissing the side of his head. The only sound in the room was our breathing and the sounds of the Christmas movie playing behind us.

After our breathing was a little more even I helped him out of bed, walking into the bathroom to turn the shower on. After getting the condom off I pulled him into a warm shower, his arms wrapping around me again. We softly swayed under the water, making me think of us softly dancing outside the bar all those months ago.

We took a well deserved shower before changing into pajamas and getting back into bed. "Do you want to restart this movie?" I whispered after realizing I had no idea what was going on.

He looked up at me with a soft smile, my thumb running over his cheek. "We can watch something else if you'd like," he said.

"I'm always down for a cheesy movie with you love." He smiled brightly, his beauty literally lighting up the entire room. "I can't wait until you're my husband one day." The shock on his face echoed how I felt. Why did I say that? "Uh, I didn't mean to make things awkward or anything."

"You didn't," he said as his eyes got misty. "You make everything right. And I'd be honored to be your husband."

He squeaked when I tackled him into a bear hug, his laughs echoing throughout the room. "I can't believe I got so lucky to end up with a cowboy."

"I'd say you're a cowboy now too."

"Cowboys forever?" I asked while holding my pinky out to him.

He laughed as he wrapped his pinky around mine. "Cowboys forever."

I got us wrapped back up in the warm blankets as he loaded up another movie. As I kissed his head I smiled, knowing the rest of my Christmases will look just like this. And there's no place I'd rather be, than down on the farm with my cowboy.

Epilogue

S even Years Later

Porter

"Uncle Levi! Can I have some more turkey?"

My eyes instantly wandered over to Paige, who was smiling brightly at Levi from her spot next to him. "Of course," he said while reaching for the plate that was in front of them. Her big green eyes followed his movements before she smiled brightly again.

"Thank you!"

"I want some more turkey," Julia said as she watcher her twin sister get more food.

"You can have more when you finish what's on your plate first," Wyatt said from the other side of the table.

Julia stared down at her plate before saying, "Okay Daddy."

A hand on my thigh made me look over at Levi, a smile instantly covering my face. A lot had changed in the past couple of years but my love for him had never changed. Since I was sitting on his left I could see his wedding ring, my fingers slowly touching it. It still feels like only yesterday that Wyatt and I were coming up the greatest plan we've ever had.

We had our dad's wedding ring split in two, the jeweler able to make two rings out of that one. The other half of Levi's ring had delicate diamonds, complimenting the silver ring my dad had. The other half of Jeremy's ring also had diamonds, mixed with some white gold. They both turned out really unique and both Jeremy and Levi had cried extremely hard.

When I proposed to Levi it was six months after our first Christmas together, when both of us were out riding horses one evening. We'd made it a tradition to ride together at least once a week, just enjoy each other's company. That particular day we rode out into the field and had a picnic, where I asked him to marry me. It was perfect and literally everything I ever wanted. Jeremy got engaged a few weeks later, when him and Wyatt went on a weekend trip. After both of our weddings Jeremy and Wyatt wasted no time in adopting their children.

When their surrogate was first pregnant no one knew she was carrying twins, a surprise to everyone. Seemed pretty fitting that an identical twin would end up having a set of identical twin girls. Paige and Julia were now six and absolutely adorable; both having green eyes and unruly blonde hair. They were the sweetest little girls I had ever been around, especially to their little brother.

My eyes wandered over to little Hudson who was now sitting on Theo's lap, his face buried into his shirt. Hudson was only three and was the shyest kid I had ever met. If he wasn't attached to either Jeremy or Wyatt, he was all over Theo. Theo and Marie were the best grandparents any child could ask for.

My eyes kept going around the table, to see Katie and her husband Patrick and their two sons Frankie and Joseph. And of course Kurt and Debbie were also at the table, their love growing stronger each and every day. They actually ended up getting married a year after Jeremy and I's weddings. It was great to see them so happy together, and to see Kurt completely healthy.

I wrapped my right arm around the back of Levi's chair, his head resting against my shoulder for a few moments. The ranch was always busy now with family, which was something I loved. All of us gathered for every holiday and every birthday. It was moments like these that I wished my dad was still here, he would have loved every minute of this. But I knew he was still here, watching over us. Hudson's middle name was also Ryan, which was our dad's name. Paige's middle name was Rachel, which was Wyatt's mother name and Julia's was Theodora, obviously named after Theo. Every single one of their names was meaningful and I thought that was beautiful.

"Would anyone like a piece of pie?" Kurt asked before starting to cut up the different pies we had. The calming sounds of everyone's voices were making me happily sigh, Levi looking back up at me.

"You okay?"

With a nod I leaned in to kiss the side of his head. "Very good. Just deciding which pie I want."

"I'd say both, they all look good."

"Amen to that," Jeremy said which made us all laugh.

The conversation switched to random topics before all the food was eventually eaten. Once the dishes were done we all watched a movie together and just had fun. I didn't think that life would have ended up like this for me, but I couldn't imagine my life to have gone any other way. Even though sometimes there are truly awful experiences in our lives, the good will come and it will find us. Mainly when we least expect it. As my eyes traveled around the room with my family I smiled, glad that I never gave up on the good in life.